T0196242

# ROCKING CHAIR CONFESSIONS

*Tales Told by a Texan
—Some Partially True!*

## Delbert "Delby" Pape

iUniverse, Inc.
Bloomington

**Rocking Chair Confessions**
**Tales Told by a Texan … Some Partially True!**

iUniverse books may be ordered through booksellers or by contacting:

iUniverse
1663 Liberty Drive
Bloomington, IN 47403
www.iuniverse.com
1-800-Authors (1-800-288-4677)

ISBN: 978-1-4759-4644-4 (sc)
ISBN: 978-1-4759-4645-1 (hc)
ISBN: 978-1-4759-4646-8 (e)

Library of Congress Control Number: 2012915677

Printed in the United States of America

iUniverse rev. date: 9/4/2012

What do you share with others? What do you reveal to a few?
What do you keep a secret?

# Dedications and Rememberances

This book is dedicated to my parents Raymond (Nickname-Jack) and Verba Pape. Also to my brothers (Ray, Wes, Jack, and Eddie) and my sisters (Deloras and Sharita) who shaped my life and made me what I am (I have to blame someone!).

This family prepared me for my sweet, loving, positive and humorous wife, Linda-a gal who giggles at any and everything. Our love brought forth five wonderful children: Peter, Lisa, Andy, Jace, and Ben. I thank her parents, Ruth and Ira Ward, for her.

I want to remember my closest *growing up* friends; Morgan, Richard, and Randy. My Cushman and Honda S-90 motor cycle running around buds from the 60's.

I remember Randy and I were riding our S-90's side-by-side one Friday night along the main drag (Sherwood Way) in San Angelo, Texas. As we were talking back and forth, I guess Randy didn't see the car in front stopping to make a right turn, as he went flying over the motorcycle handle bars. Randy landed on the trunk of the car, slid up the back window, and landed on top of the small Corvair vehicle. What a sight! I wish I'd had my instamatic camera.

I especially want to remember my college friend and *best man* at my wedding, Steve. We had some fun college times and enjoyed chillin' to the Bee Gee's.

I'd like to say hi to Debbie, Susan, Sandy, and Edith.

Hello also to Tascha, I hope your enjoying your zoo career. Linda and I miss you at our movie night of popcorn, drinks, and stories.

I can't forget Helen, the manager of the *Charcoal House* (great hamburgers and steak fingers!) all those years I worked there as a teen. She fired me several times only to rehire me a few days later. A patient woman indeed.

# Forward

Have you ever found yourself on your morning run waving, as you crossed paths, to a complete stranger and then caught yourself wondering what stories they <u>could</u> or <u>would</u> tell you?

Maybe you were riding on a public transportation system from the airport and as you peered out the window to experience the city, you noticed the many faces that were different yet somehow familiar. You pondered and exclaimed within yourself, "they too have stories to tell."

Did you sit for hours in shallow conversation with college friends and walk away thinking, "we really didn't say much…did we?"

What or how would you react if, on your 21st birthday, you sat down with your parents as you had so many times before and they informed you that you were adopted by them in your infancy?

How would you react if, as you and your spouse are watching television, your spouse turned off the television set and announced that he had a child from a previous relationship many years ago! Or, what if the child showed up on your doorstep and made the announcement?

As a child, I was not wise to my adult world of parents and aunts and uncles and the like. But I did get bits and pieces of stories that I eventually pieced together, with the help of family and friends, as I grew into the adulthood world. I was fascinated at what I later learned.

I have pieced together 23 short stories that have some elements of actual events, but for the most part are fictitious. And although these stories are, by and large, fiction; they could have in reality happened to someone…maybe someone like you!

# Contents

# Introduction

I recently attended a family reunion in Barksdale, Texas. At only thirteen months of age, my youngest grandaughter took hold of my finger and led me around the Mary B. Powers Hall building, past the tennis courts, around the school, and back. Upon our return, she began zigzagging in different directions across the grassy area where we have our famous family reunion "washer tournament," which fortunately had not gotten under way just yet. I kept thinking how aimless our walk was—back and forth and back again.

She would take a high step and get up on the cemented sidewalk, giggle, and then take another high step back down onto the grass, and then she would giggle again as she looked up at me. She was having a *heck* of a good time. Watching her and seeing the expressions on her face made me realize that this was not an aimless walk at all but a very adventurous walk indeed!

Before you are twenty-three short stories. I hope you will not view them as an aimless walk but will experience each as a true adventure!

Delbert Doyce Pape
Baytown, Texas
August 2012

# Hello, Will You Marry Me?

*Have you ever entered a wrong number on your phone,*
*and it turned out to be the best thing you ever did?*

Hello, my name is Richard E. Montgomery. The *E* stands for Edgar, which I'm not crazy about but am very proud to have, as it was given to me by my father on behalf of his father. In other words, it's a family name from my grandfather. I was not privileged to meet this man, but I heard many entertaining stories about him. … But that's another story for another time.

Now, back in the old days, not everyone had a telephone. My family didn't have one, but we did have access to the town drugstore phone for free (local) calls during store hours. "Old Man Jones" and his wife, Zelda, were the owners of the store, which had a small eating area and a book section called Poppy Emporium. They were the model of good neighbors. If you had an emergency after store hours—and even if you didn't—Old Man Jones would be more than willing to open up the store and let you in to use the phone—but not after 9:00 p.m. or after dark, whichever came first. It was nice that way since they lived in the back part of the store and were almost always home except for once a year when they took a vacation during the latter part of July.

Two years after I graduated from high school, I was working at the drugstore part-time as well as working the family farm the other time. I had been seeing a very attractive girl by the name of Arzeal. I liked her a lot, but I got busy with the two jobs. About three months earlier was our last time together. Previously, I met and had a few dates with Leona, a brunette of about five feet six inches tall and very witty. Leona and Arzeal were friends (not best friends, but still friends), and they lived a few miles out of town, about half a mile apart. The girls had gone to school with each other until their graduation a few months before, and they still visited from time to time.

I was just piddling around the store—you know, straightening things up and wiping down the counters. Ralph came in and ordered a sandwich with all the fixings. We were old buds; we used to play pranks in our school days. I'm sure all the teachers celebrated on my graduation day, and especially when Ralph decided not to return to school the following fall.

Ralph was a year behind me in school, and I hadn't seen him in about that long. When he left school, he had gotten a job on a ranch north of town, close to Amarillo. Wow! And here he was back. We shared story after story of the past year and numerous stories of our high school days while I filled orders for other customers. This was good for me and just as good for Ralph.

Before I knew it, two hours had gone by with the listening customers all glad to see Ralph. They welcomed him back heartily. They even threw in a few stories of their own about us and the locals. We laughed and then all cried when we related about how Jimmy Short had lost his life in just an old friendly fight when he was knocked down by an upper cut from his buddy, Justin Barlow.

Justin had taken a few good licks and then got in a good upper cut and knocked Jimmy backward. That sent him back, and as he was trying to gain his balance step by step, he fell to the ground headfirst. He landed on a board with a long nail protruding from it. We all thought Jimmy was either knocked out or playing possum. He didn't move at first, but then he moaned and began to flop around in the area, after which he lay still—never to move again. Justin was the first to race over to assist him. Then, after a few suggestions, we carried him over to Doc Whithers's place. After we related what had happened, Doc showed us out. Shortly afterward, Doc pronounced him dead. We all just cried for hours.

It seemed such a waste of a life for a little fun and entertainment. A friendly fight was not too uncommon for our little town, at least among the youth. A little innocent fight, and no one was mad. No one blamed Justin. We felt sorry for him more than anything and even more sorry for Jimmy. We eventually got somewhat over it, but we still missed our friend whose life was cut short.

A few weeks later, I was thinking about our little get-together—"story time" with Ralph and me and our friends. I began to think about Leona and Arzeal. For the first time, I began thinking about marriage, settling down, having kids, and raising a family. I was doing well and had saved some money. I also knew the farm was going to be mine. Maybe it's the "out of sight, out of mind" thing with Arzeal since Leona was the most recent girl I had dated. Next thing I knew, I was phoning Leona's home. She answered, but the connection was a little on the staticky side. Through the static, we talked about how much we missed each other. I hinted about marriage, family, and the like and asked her to come into town so I could ask her something. We hung up. There was no question about the "question" I was going to ask her—and she knew it too.

You need to know something about the phones back then. Rural phones had no dials for dialing. A receiver and speaker piece on a box hanging on a wall was it. Each house had its own special ring and was rung by a phone operator. To get the operator, one grabbed a rotary handle on the side of the wall phone and wound it around, sending a ringing signal to the operator. Leona's was two long rings and two short rings, and the drugstore's was three long and one short. Arzeal was three long and three short. I remember a little later the rotary phones coming in style where one could put a finger in an opening with a number from zero through nine, then "rotate" or dial a sequence of numbers. Each house had a series of numbers assigned to it.

Party lines were the norm. A party line was a line shared by two or more households, and if someone was on the phone at one home, those in another home would have to wait until the line was free-unless they wanted to listen in, which of course was considered very inconsiderate. Private lines came later and of course cost more to those who wanted them.

Private lines eventually became the standard as did also the push-button phones. Cell phones are the current wave and are here to stay. It took me a while to get to the point to purchase one. I actually got it for Christmas from my grandchildren who are wonderful and a joy in my life. They keep me young and make sure I am familiar with the modern technologies. Why just the other day, they taught me how to use my DVD player to record my favorite movies and shows on disk. ... Oh, pardon me, I need to get back to my story.

I was busy cleaning up for closing and waiting for Leona, hoping to be done by the time she was to arrive. Yes, it was almost 6:30—closing time for this one-horse town. (*One horse* is a figure of speech that means "small"—not much going on or to do.) I had a jar of mustard in my hand and was headed for the small cooler vault in the back when it slipped out of my hand. The reason it slipped was because I was goosed from behind by someone. Reaching for the falling mustard jar, I went down with it and ended up cutting my hand. As I got myself up I could see ... Arzeal? Arzeal was standing there!

"Arzeal! What are you doing here?" was all I could gasp. Well, she giggled and made fun of my clumsiness but also wanted to know if I was hurt and if everything was okay. She seemed overly friendly at the time, which I understood a little later on. After a few minutes more of chitchat, I began to realize why I so enjoyed her company. Her dark eyes, tall build, and cute smile started it all over for me. But I think it was her accentuated southern drawl that was more pronounced than most in this neck of the woods. Finally, she asked me.

Arzeal blurted it out right there. "Well, Richard E. Montgomery, what did you call me down here to ask me?" *Oh, brother!* I said to myself with surprise. It dawned on me in a flash what had happened. When I had earlier thought I called for Leona, I'd ended up calling Arzeal. I could only theorize that the operator had rung the wrong number or something like that. Well, we pussyfooted around for a while longer, talking about this and that. And it may be hard to accept unless you have experienced it for yourself, but I fell in love with her. Yes, sir, I made up my mind to ask her to marry me. And I did, right then and there. I was never more sure of myself than I was at that moment. And I was never happier than when she began to cry, with "yes" splattered all over her lips.

Well, sir, I told you it would be hard to believe. But it happened just that way, at least as I recall it.

We celebrated our fifty-seventh wedding anniversary last August with our twenty grandchildren, seven great-grandchildren, and our five wonderful children: Peter, Lisa, Andy, Jace, and Ben. Arzeal is now in a rest home close by, and I visit her almost every day, when I'm not sick. I can honestly say I have kept this story of how we got together to myself for all these years, but this Saturday, I'll let the secret escape from my lips to Azeal's ears. I don't think she'll be upset. Besides, we shouldn't keep secrets from each other now, should we? She's the greatest thing that has ever happened to me—and I love her!

# Hook 'Em Horns!

*How many chances do you give others before you realize you've been taken advantage of? Mary realized this and made a very tough decision which you may or may not approve of.*

For the purpose of this narrative, I'll just call myself Mary. I was raised poor but not dirt poor. This was so until I entered junior high (or what is called middle school nowadays). Then Dad got a nice and welcomed promotion with steady—and substantial—pay increases after that. Things changed for me too, and I was voted most likely to succeed in high school. When I graduated in 1983, everything was looking good!

After college graduation, I was employed as a public relations/ marketing assistant executive in Irving, Texas. The title sounds better than the job—there were several of us assistant execs around the company. The company was involved in the construction of swimming pools, pool products, and pool servicing. It did a booming business, and it catered mostly to builders who constructed new homes and to hotels and motels. The company grew fast and so did the bonuses; I was doing well.

In January of 1988, I met Larry Bingman. He was one of the company's three VPs. He was handsome and going places, and I was going with him. Each day I fell deeper in love with him, and we married the following July. Our baby boy was born in 1991. Other than "our bundle of joy," we called him Jack. Oh yeah, we had the house, the cars, and all that goes with it, until …

We celebrated our fifth wedding anniversary at a nice restaurant, came home with some friends, and celebrated some more. The next morning we went to work as usual. At about ten o'clock, I was called to the boss's office. Mr. Ward made me comfortable and then closed the door after a police officer and a detective came in. He introduced me to Officer Benson and then to Detective Pape. Mr. Ward said these gentlemen had some news to tell me.

It was Detective Pape who broke the news that Larry had been the target of an ongoing investigation lasting several months and culminating with his arrest earlier that morning. He further explained that he had been charged with the crime of embezzlement from company funds. I couldn't look at Mr. Ward the rest of the interview. They asked me a few more questions and decided I didn't have any knowledge of the goings-on. I was released and told where to find my husband.

With Larry in prison, I was barely able to make it on my own with just my pay. Mom and Dad were killed in an automobile accident a year later, and the inheritance money pulled little Jack and me through with what would have been even tougher times. Larry in prison, losing my parents—it was all I could take. But finally, Larry was out. Three long years, and he was back.

We went through an adjustment phase because I had grown fairly independent. That was hard on Larry, but it was nothing compared to his stubbornness. Prison had given him a hard heart against the world. I could see he had not taken rehabilitation very well. I had started going to church with Jack when Larry was in prison, but Larry would have nothing to do with it now.

On the other hand, Larry would have everything to do with alcohol. It was his friend. He couldn't find employment—or wouldn't, is more like it. Months went by when I finally found that with Larry's drinking, and now drugs, he was spending us into the poorhouse if it didn't stop. Creditors were hounding us—actually, *me*! Larry denied the bills at first until the excuses fell apart by way of reasoning. Then I caught him with another woman! I had gone through a lot. This was just too much!

Before I could get divorce papers filed, Larry was diagnosed with brain cancer. My insurance kept us afloat financially on that one. Over a two-year period, he was hospitalized four times. Each time the doctors said it was the end, and four times they were wrong! When he was in the hospital was when I felt the most peaceful.

At home, Larry was depressed, rarely interacted with us, and tried to argue a lot. I learned early that it takes two to argue. He even called other people to argue with. I finally disconnected his cell phone services. He couldn't figure out why his phone didn't work, although I had told him several times about my disconnecting it. His brain wasn't functioning correctly ... not firing on all cylinders—know what I mean?

My work gave me rest and I excelled. I didn't continue to pursue the divorce as planned, although in hindsight I should have. There was something about his getting cancer that wouldn't let me go through with it. I should not have listened to *that* voice. Church services, which once gave me such comfort, now left me cold. The pastor, once warm and understanding, now seemed more interested in my collection plate offerings or tithing donations. Lately, his sermons were centered more on donations from the congregation members than on worshipping God.

Four o'clock one morning, I was awakened by a thud and a lamp being knocked over. Larry was up as usual at all hours of the night. He had fallen out of his wheelchair and hit his head on the edge of an end table. As I approached him, I could see a cut on his neck caused by the broken glass from the lamp. If I could get him to the hospital, I figured he'd be all right—but I didn't.

I went upstairs and got back into bed. Thirty minutes later, I went back downstairs. He was still breathing but unconscious. I hesitated and then slowly walked over and picked up a piece of the broken lamp and made the cut in his neck a little deeper. Ten more minutes went by and then thirty minutes. Forty-five minutes later, I called the emergency number. The ambulance arrived shortly. Larry was pronounced dead as they raced to the hospital. I cried—not for Larry, but for my own mental well-being. I was exhausted … and relieved.

Months went by, and no cops. Then years came and went, and no arrest. Nothing but good came to Jack and me from that moment on. A few months later, the pastor came by to invite me back to church as if I were a wayward sheep or lost puppy. He reminded me about the Trinity of God and his love for me, and that he is always there to help. I blurted out, "How could they be one? Was God praying to himself in the garden? Was he going to sit on "his" own right-hand side of "himself" in heaven? And why is there no mention of Jesus outside of the Bible during his supposed time on earth?" He could only cough up that it was all a mystery; we must all believe by faith. I showed him the door and stated, "I want knowledge so I can be on sure ground like a rock and not sink in the sand." He left and I've not heard from him to this day. I did get that knowledge that leads to a more sure word of understanding. That's another story.

When Jack graduated from college, I remarried and have a wonderful husband. James is a professor at the University of Texas. Jack is a successful engineer with Exxon and has a beautiful wife and three children. What a proud mom I am as James and I attend various Longhorn functions and activities. Hook 'em Horns!

# My Baby

*Teacher alert! You may have wanted to do something like this teacher did ... but don't try it.*

I coached high school football for ten years and then decided to hang it up and teach full-time. I enjoyed coaching for the first five years, but it became boring—the same goals each year, doing the same thing practice after practice, not to mention the politics and parents. Eventually, at the end of year ten, I taught social studies full-time and enjoyed it for another twenty-one years. Then I retired. The kids and association with the school were an added bonus—with the exception of one student in particular.

I met David Walter the first day of school in 1983 in first period. He was a freshman and new to Wiggins High. Our school was called the Wiggins Weasels, and we had "weaseled" our way to state AAA football champs in 1981. All David could do was talk football, although he had never played for the school. When it came to schoolwork, he was the first to complain that the work was too much, or he'd lay his head down, claiming a headache. Sometimes, I'd give him an alternate assignment to help him succeed. He disliked school and everything associated with it, except sports and bothering others. David's grades reflected his attitude.

Following basic teaching 101, I tried to ignore his negative behavior, hoping it would go away; it didn't. Later in the year, David started his prank mode. He would put gum in student chairs; shoot rubber bands across the room and deny it came from him; and more than once, he smeared ink on the door handle to classrooms, mine included. He was dumb enough to not realize that hall cameras caught him each time. At one point, it did occur to him to cover one of those cameras, but the camera showed him approaching with the handkerchief to cover it. He must have liked in-school suspension (ISS) for his punishment because he was there a lot.

David came from a somewhat well-to-do family financially. The parents were well liked in the community of Wiggins, Oklahoma. His father had built up a flourishing family business in the housing construction sector. Wiggins was a growing community, and so was the construction world. Those teachers and others who knew David would kid about how his father had worked hard to build up his company, and yet David would not be bright enough to be able to take it over and continue its success. But his mother was the tree, and David was the fruit that didn't fall far from her nitwittedness.

Don't be led into thinking David was a pill in my class only. It stretched into each classroom he was associated with. My dealings with his mother, Sara, were comical. At a parent/teacher conference we had, she displayed the intelligence of a flea. She would claim her boy would "never do something like that." Then she would go into a story about something that David had done at home, which ended up being more revolting than the shenanigan he'd pulled in my class (and thus the reason for the conference).

David was a fighter. I mean he really liked to get into fights, which he did fairly often. Usually he came out on top. They were mostly after school and not on school property, which meant he didn't get into school trouble over that aspect of his life. He would tell me of his after-school fights and his other interests during detention time. I got sucked into going the extra mile with him, but toward the end of the school year, I knew I was being taken for a ride and I wised up.

I had, at least in the beginning, given David a lot of extra leeway in his unruly behavior. I even fudged a passing grade one six-week period, which helped him pass the semester—you know, giving him the benefit of the doubt. Well, I shouldn't have, I now realize. He just took advantage of it and goofed off even more the next semester.

Why was I trying so hard to give him extra time to complete his assignments and extra assistance during early-morning and after-school tutorials? I even sought him out and got him to come to tutorials. He liked coming to my room early in the mornings because few students would sit with him before school. But after a short while, he began disrupting tutorials; he had to go!

School was only two weeks from letting out. One afternoon about fifteen minutes after school, I noticed a student by my car. I could see through the glass doors into the parking spaces while I stretched in my classroom doorway. I went outside, then noticed it was David and went over to talk to him. When I asked him what he was doing in the teacher parking area, he went into how he admired my car.

I will admit I had a nice car. It was a Chevrolet Corvette—yellow, black interior with a removable see-through tinted glass top. It was "my baby," and I babied it. After a short talk and showing David the interior, I reminded him not to come into the teacher parking lot again. After escorting David out of the parking lot, I returned to my classroom, completed a few things, and left for the day.

As I approached *my baby*, I saw that the car next to mine was gone and a scratch that appeared to have been made by a key was exposed on the left side. I was hot—mad! No! Madder than that—madder than a hornet! I knew immediately now why David had been in that area. Not only my car, I found out later, but two others as well were scratched up. Nothing could be done, the principal told us, since no one actually saw him do it, and he denied it anyway. *What a deal*, I thought in disgust. *He got away with another one; the little dirtbag.*

Well, here it was, the last day of school. All the exams had been given, and I was one of four teachers with the duty to stay a few hours after to ensure all students vacated the premises. Most had left, and then a fight broke out between, who else, David and another student. The other student ran off as I grabbed David. We walked inside the school, down the hall, and to the principal's office. The principal was away from his desk and almost everyone else was gone.

As we sat there, I thought of the problems this student had put on me all year. I especially thought of the scratch he recently put on my car. Suddenly, I jumped up and told David to follow me. We went to my classroom. I kept thinking, *No one is around; almost everyone is gone. There's nobody here but David and me.* I told David that we'd wait here for the principal so I could finish up some last-minute schoolwork.

"David, remember when we studied about the inhabitants of Australia and how in some of the pictures they wore big smiles on their faces?" He agreed, but I knew, and he knew, he didn't remember. So I asked him to smile like they smiled. He played right along and gave a big smile.

"No, no, no, David. You need to be standing." So he stood. I squared with him, reared back, and punched him right in the kisser. I could hear a tooth crunch. Then I grabbed hold of his shirt around the chest area, pinned him to the wall, and hit him again. I thought he would fall, but he didn't—he was tough. I reminded him that I knew it was "*you*" who put the scratch on *my* car. I hit him once more and felt his legs buckle as he slid down the wall to the floor. I felt great! He didn't.

When he could walk, I escorted him outside and reminded him I knew what he had done to my car. I even told him I'd not report the fight to the principal. "Just go home." As he departed, I said, "We're square now." He didn't say a word. Later that day, just to cover myself, I told Mr. Stark my version of the story—at least all that happened outside between David and the other student. We agreed not to pursue any other discipline as long as the parents didn't complain, and besides, it was the last day of school with senior graduation tomorrow night.

The following fall, school began again. This would be my last year and then retirement. I was looking forward to this one. Mr. Stark pulled me over to the side on day one and related how David's mother had called him the next week after the fight last school year. How she said that David claimed that I had hit him. "I simply reminded her of your integrity and professionalism," he said, "and then she related how her David had a wild imagination and lied a lot. She even apologized for the phone call."

I wondered what it was going to be like this year. David was a sophomore now. I would see him in the hall from time to time. Each time we passed, he greeted me with great respect—more than I got the entire previous year. Yes, I think I taught him more in those few moments than in all of his previous year in my class. My last year was wonderful and I am now enjoying my retirement years.

# A Greatly Appreciated Gift

*Surprises are fun to get, especially if you wanted the gift for a long time but thought you'd never in a million years get it.*

Living in Odessa, Texas was a hoot in the 1930s. Hi, I'm Leah Deets, and I was a child of the Depression-era thirties. We went through hard times; we all did. It's easier when everyone is in the same boat, and a loving family helped a lot, too. The big problems come when one is poor but all the others around are well off. That wasn't the case in the Depression thirties.

I recall a Depression snack my mom used to make that really tasted very good. It was oatmeal that was cooked in a small amount of butter with sugar added. We learned how to make do and to use and reuse everything. Children would entertain themselves with hide-and-seek, tag, and board games. My parents would sit on the front porch and rock while we played tag well past dark and then played hide-and-seek with fireflies flying around us. The economy eventually improved as time went by.

Well, I grew up and got married to a wonderful man named Burton. Burt was smart, witty, and had a good head for farming. We had a nice house, and there was a second smaller house on acreage about a stone's throw away where Burt's parents had raised him (it's empty now). Ours was a two-bedroom house with five rooms in all. We raised a few chickens and had some cows. Burt would hunt deer, dove, and quail. I would go with him and hunt, too, from time to time.

A lot of German stock had settled in West Texas and realized the area was short on rainfall, so they created "tanks." Tanks were created by identifying the lowest spot on the acreage of land, and then pushing dirt together and shaping it in such a way as to accumulate or otherwise collect rain and rain runoff. Pretty smart thinking. We had a large tank which provided water for the farm animals and a well for us. The tank was also stocked with fish—mostly catfish and perch.

We'd been married about four years and finally realized we couldn't have children, as related by the country doctor. About that time, a poor family moved in with four children and no husband. Our pastor told us about them and asked if they could stay on our place in the small, empty house behind us. We met Dehava and the children, and agreed.

To help Dehava, I paid her to do our laundry as she also took in others' laundry as well. We'd go to church in our 1938 Ford flatbed farm truck since it could hold all of us. Dehava would make the laundry exchanges to the other members without any trouble.

Once in a while, Burt and I would have Dehava and the kids over for a fish fry. Sometimes we'd invite neighbors when we had a big catch and needed to get the catfish population down. Paul and Eileen Wilson would supply the cantelope and okra. Other neighbors supplied apple and other various pies.

Dehava had an especially charming boy named Harlon. He was dark-haired and blue-eyed. I really took a liking to him. We would sit together in church, and we'd cut up. When Dehava would bring the laundry over, she would bring Harlon along. I'd pay her and send a pie home with them.

One evening, Burton and I took a stroll around the farm. This was typical of our together time when we would talk and discuss. On this day, we walked a little further, all the way to my sister and her family. We spent some time with Ethel and her kids, and then her husband, Ed, came in from farming peanuts. Her kids just reminded me of my natural fondness for children. I did so wish for children.

Six months later, I got the surprise of my life. Pastor Jackson appeared at my door and stated that Dehava had come to him yesterday morning and dropped off all her children. She said she was going back to Kansas and start her life over—and off she went. Pastor stated she gave instructions on what to do with her children. Pastor Jackson said he tried to talk her out of it, but her mind was steadfast. She had not come to this decision overnight but with lots of thought.

The biggest surprise was when the pastor called Harlon over to where we were. He got out of the car and ran to me with a big country smile and a hug. Harlon was to be mine!

Well, we raised Harlon as our own, and a fine son he was. He excelled in school and was a pitcher on the high school baseball team. He pitched a no-hitter one playoff game and got his picture in the paper all the way to Abilene, Texas. We still have our family get-togethers every July with Harlon and his wife, Tiffany, and their four wonderful children: Randy, Elizabeth, Tammy, and Linda. Now let me tell you about my grandchildren …

# That's My Necklace!

*Have you ever solved an actual criminal case
by watching television? Carol did.*

C arol. My name is Carolyn but most call me Carol or just "C." I grew up in Missoula, Montana. I loved it there. One of my best memories is when the singer Anne Murray came there a time or two to put on a performance, and I would go with my parents. Anne delivered a fantastic show.

Eventually, I graduated from nursing school in 1978. The 1980s were good to me. After graduation I was hired on at a small general hospital in Kalispell, Montana. I sure did enjoy working at that place. The people were great—laid back and easy going. The community was about twenty-five thousand, had a mall, and there were lots of friendly faces. Eddie was one of them.

Eddie and I spent a lot of time together. He seemed to have a never-ending supply of money. We had many good times boating on Flathead Lake and running around in Lakeside, which was only twenty miles from Kalispell. At Lakeside, there used to be a military radar site—Air Force, I think—on Blacktail Mountain. I heard the military turned it over to the FAA later.

Just a few miles further was a nice restaurant called The Tammarack. It had the best steaks I've ever tasted. They'd come out with the steak, and it was three-fourths of an inch thick; it covered the entire plate (and lapped over the edge). The vegetables and the rest of the dinner were served on another smaller plate. I never could eat the whole thing, but I did get another great meal the next day all right!

Sometimes Eddie's parents would come down from Big Fork. We'd take them to The Tammarack and get a seat next to one of the bay windows with a spectacular view of Flathead Lake, which made the food taste that much better. The lake was beautiful in the summer, and we even did some ice fishing in the winter. I only went a couple of times—it was just too cold. I'll leave ice fishing to the guys. I sure have a lot of fond memories of Kalispell.

In 1989, I moved to Great Falls, Montana. I was hired on at the regional hospital there and promoted to assistant head nurse five years later. Didn't see Eddie anymore other than once when he came to visit. I had a few letters and a couple of phone calls at the beginning, but nothing after the visit. So, during his visit, I gave him back the locket he had given me earlier. I did this just to see if it was really over. It was.

Shortly after Eddie left, I met Wesley. Wes was a patient at the hospital, and we hit it off just fine. He was in for a hernia operation. Our personalities fit together like hand and glove. Six months later, we got married. I had just turned thirty-seven, and he was forty-five.

Wes was a regional rep for Yellow Front food stores, a grocery and miscellaneous store scattered throughout most of the north to northwestern area of the States. He had started out as a stocker twenty-three years earlier after a three-year tour with the Navy. He was smart, and his hard work was rewarded accordingly with numerous promotions. He had been promoted to regional rep three years before I met him. Wes always said he was one of those promoted on merit and not on who he knew or was related to. That was no reflection on the company, mind you. It was just his way of saying he felt he had worked for his promotions, whereas some hadn't.

I didn't know much about what Wes did day to day at Yellow Front, so a few months before he was to retire, the company had a "spouse day." Each spouse was invited to an open house–type get-together at company headquarters and would "shadow" their spouse around all or part of the day. Toward the end of the spouse day, we went on a guided tour through the company memorabilia. It consisted of two rooms on the east wing of the main floor. At the end of a newspaper display, I was drawn to an article about a robbery that occurred at Yellow Front corporate offices.

It had a video one could play of the robbery caught on camera. I pressed the button for it to play and watched a hooded man making his theft. Couldn't tell much, but I did notice a necklace around the neck of the robber. I looked closer, but it was not clear enough to tell anything. The company president walked over and stated they had never caught him.

He pointed out the necklace and said the robber dropped it before his getaway. He fast-forwarded it to that place so he could show me when it fell. The camera showed the robber unconsciously grabbing his neck, but he was not aware it had fallen off. Then the robber went on about his business. The president then announced to the gathered group that *Unsolved Mysteries* was going to carry a television segment about the robbery the first Wednesday of the following month, if anyone was interested.

I went home and looked up the listing on the Internet and marked my calendar. I thought this would be fun and exciting as it related to something Wes and I were familiar with. I think—no, I know—I was more excited than Wes. On the night of the airing I made some popcorn, got our drinks, and we settled on the couch in front of our sixty-five-inch TV screen. We were set!

Ours was the second segment of the show. It started with a brief history of the crime and some narrative with actors reenacting the story that had been gathered over the years, and then they showed the same video clip that was shown at the spouse day. At the end, the host stated that the necklace had an inscription on it which said, "To: C–From: Eddie."

"That's mine!" I shouted. "It's Eddie! Eddie did it. That was the locket he gave me, and I returned to him. It's him!" I was almost hysterical. No, I was hysterical! As I came to my senses, I saw popcorn and the popcorn bowl strewn on the carpeted floor. I hurriedly grabbed a pen and waited for the number to come on the screen.

I gave the operator all I knew. Eventually, I was interviewed three more times, and then after that I provided a statement. Seven months later, I got a call from the company president, and he stated that the detectives followed up on my lead, and when confronted with all the evidence and a witness who would testify about the locket, Eddie had folded and confessed. The president expressed his appreciation, and we received a nice reward from the company.

Later, Eddie tried to withdraw his confession, but through a plea bargain agreement, he settled for twelve years. He is on his third year and will probably get out sometime after his sixtieth birthday, if I calculated right. I researched the robbery and found that Eddie had committed the theft when he came to visit me that one time just before we officially broke up. And I didn't even suspect it until I saw *Unsolved Mysteries*.

On a later episode of the show, they showed a rerun of the first showing with an update. I was featured with a thirty-second spot for my role in the capture of "Eddie the Bandit." The show ended with the host declaring that "Eddie the Bandit" is under wraps thanks to courageous people like Carol, a.k.a. "C" as she is known affectionately by us and not so affectionately by Eddie."

# My Most Forgettable Alaskan Tour

*There's a lot of "cold" in those Alaskan hills.*

In 1973, I completed three years with the United States Air Force and was just checking into a remote radar site called Sparrevohn. The site was perched atop a mountain about 175 miles west of Anchorage, Alaska. The only way to get to Sparrevohn Air Station was by aircraft. No roads, in or out, went there! I arrived via helicopter and was very impressed with the scenery as we helicoptered through the mountain pass before arriving at Sparrevohn from Anchorage. I was going to be there for twelve months.

I was a technician in a radar tower with a crew that maintained the radar and ancillary equipment associated with it. The winters were long and cold with up to twenty-three hours of darkness during the dead of winter. The opposite was true during the summer. Our days were filled with lots of Ping-Pong and card playing. We'd have a Ping-Pong tournament most weekends.

To keep the morale up, we got heaps of the best food around. Every Sunday at dinner, we were served steak and lobster with all the trimmings. Ummmm ... it was good. There was always peach cobbler or cake left out all through the weekend to snack on as we championed for bragging rights for "Ping-Pong champion of the week" player. I faired pretty good and took my share of winning the weekly title. What else could we do? It got close to minus one hundred degrees outside sometimes.

On the other hand, the summers were nice for a very short while. We'd get out and break the cabin-fever spell by taking a walk. Richard, Randy, and I did stuff together. Sometimes, we just sat along the mountainside and talked. Numerous times we saw birds, three times we saw a moose, and several times a fox. It was the same fox each time as it knew where to come for a free and easy meal.

Richard was from Gary, Indiana. He was the cautious one. When we were going for a walk, he was the one telling us we'd better not go too far. Then he'd be the one wanting to go and observe this or that to fulfill his curiosity. He was a lot different than Randy.

Randy was from Lafayette, Louisiana—a Cajun. He was cool. He taught us some things about Cajun lingo. He would tell us stories about his trips to The Big Easy, which is a nickname for New Orleans, meaning "to take it easy" or "to be easy going." He had a million stories about Mardi Gras. He told us that Mardi Gras means Fat Tuesday and is the day before Ash Wednesday (usually in February or March), so it's the last day to party before Lent. For those who participate, Lent is when one gives something up for forty days (from Ash Wednesday up to Easter) to show a willingness to sacrifice something of value to oneself. I just liked to hear the way he talked when he told us these things.

Once, I was downhearted and expressed how I missed my family. Randy overheard me and poked his head in my direction and said, "C'est la vie." Then he told me that it meant "that's life." After that, he went down the hall with his goofy laugh that always made me feel better.

When we'd sit down to eat, he would tell us "bon appétit," meaning "good appetite" or "enjoy." More than once, he relayed to us how he missed cochon de lait (koh SHON duh lay). We'd ask him what that was, and he'd tell us it was a whole suckling pig roasted over an open flame. "Sounds good to me," we all said at the same time. Then he would rejoin with, "Stop the gumbo ya ya."

"What's that you say … gumbo ya ya?" we'd ask.

Randy would explain that it's when several people talk at once. Then he would go into his goofy laugh.

During Christmas, we got a nice break with a visit from a small Eskimo village located twenty-five miles away. We, the military site, sponsored the entire village by having them over for a Christmas feast with presents for the little tikes. Almost the entire village was flown in and back by military aircraft for this special community-building experience. A total of seventy to eighty Eskimo-Alaskans attended. Some were full Eskimo or part, and many had married Americans or Canadians. They stayed about four days, and then returned with presents. We all had a wonderful experience together and enough stories to last until next year; they all had strong views on the Alaska Native Claims Settlement Act.

Master Sergeant Wendle Johnson was our shop leader (noncommissioned officer in charge). He was a trooper! Best boss I ever had. He had only two years left for retirement, and then he was going to start a Christmas tree farm in Minnesota. That guy was strong and knew how to hike long distances. For a person forty-three years old, he showed us younger troops a thing or two.

One day, he announced he was going to hike to the Eskimo village and come back over the weekend and asked if anyone wanted to go with him. He got no takers so he headed out alone. Before leaving, he asked me to help him pack food for his hike. We culled over some food the cook said we could go through. I packed some canned fruit and found a couple of cans of tuna fish, then I put a can opener in while he snagged a few more items and called it good. I wished him well, and off he went as he stated he'd see us Sunday late afternoon.

Well, Sunday afternoon rolled around and no Wendle Jones. Later that evening, the site commander seemed concerned as he asked over the intercom system if anyone had heard from Master Sergeant Jones. No one had heard anything. The commander announced that the village had been contacted and that Jones had left with enough time for him to have returned by now.

Eventually, higher headquarters was notified and a search party authorized, organized, and sent out. Afterward, the sergeant's body was found and sent to Anchorage, Alaska. I left Sparrevohn one month later and was assigned to Duluth International Airport, Minnesota. More importantly, I was back with my family.

I didn't hear anything more about Sparrevohn until six months later when I overheard a conversation between two officers at the base barbershop while I was waiting my turn to have my hair cut. I could only get bits and pieces of the conversation and really wasn't paying too much attention until "Sparrevohn" came up in the talk. Then I heard one of the officers say that a Master Sergeant Jones had gone hiking and was found dead. The autopsy showed hyperthermia as the cause of death, but that food poisoning from a can of tuna fish contributed. The expiration date on the can was thirteen months past, and had it not been for the tuna, he probably would have survived. I felt sick.

I know I shouldn't blame myself, but I sure do wish I had checked the tuna expiration date on the can. If you ever see me on the street, you can invite me in for coffee, donuts, or a burger and fries, but don't ever offer me anything having to do with tuna fish!

# Zozobra and Ray, or Ramon, or Whatever

*Hey, I have some oceanfront property in Arizona and New Mexico to sell, real cheap.*

B orn, bred, and grew up in Santa Fe, New Mexico. I was raised in a family of eight children, and I was number seven. I was christened Manuel Ramon Gaudalupe Hernando Chanchez. I went by "Ramon" most of my youth, and now everyone, except Lucinda-my wife, calls me Ray. As she told me one time, "You were Ramon when I married you, and Ramon you'll always be."

Lucinda was traditional, and I wouldn't want her any other way. She loved living in Santa Fe, and I knew she'd never leave. She had been a Harvey Girl for several years until we met and got married.

Mr. Harvey retired high up in the railroad business and had some restaurant experience as well. In 1870, Fred Harvey started his push to bring good food at reasonable prices in clean, elegant restaurants, to the public throughout the Southwest. At its peak, he operated eighty-four Harvey Houses.

By the late 1950s, the railroads were worn out by years of carrying war goods, and as the business world and public were then relying on other modes of transportation, they began cutting back. The passenger trains started to decline as well. Most railroads were eliminating services, but the Santa Fe was one of the holdouts; eventually, it too succumbed. Fewer passengers and travelers meant that Lucinda was out of work.

Santa Fe is a festive city, and Fiestas have been celebrated since 1712, while the burning of Zozobra started in 1926. Zozobra is a hideous but harmless twenty-foot (or thirty- or forty- or fifty-foot, depending on who you talk to) boogey-man marionette. He is toothless, he moans and groans, rolls his eyes, and twists his head. His mouth gapes open and chomps while his arms flail about in frustration. Every year, we string Zozobra up and set him ablaze with fireworks. At last he is done in, taking with him all our troubles for another year.

The Kiwanis Club has been involved in the Zozobra event for some few decades, and it is a fiery and exciting kickoff to the annual Fiestas de Santa Fe during the weekend following Labor Day. After the burning of Zozobra, the band strikes up "La Cucaracha." Afterward, the crowd marches back between bonfires along the streets to the armory and the big festivities are on!

In 1869, construction on the Saint Frances Cathedral began. The cathedral was built on the site of an adobe church that was destroyed in the Pueblo Revolt. Portions of the old adobe parish church (La Parroquia) remain in the form of the chapel of Our Lady of the Rosary. La Conquistadora (a wooden statue of the Virgin) is housed there. It was first brought to Santa Fe in 1625 and was returned by the armies of Don Diego de Vargas during the reconquest of 1692–1693.

To finish my short story, Santa Fe is the oldest capital city in the United States and the oldest European community in America west of the Mississippi. The Palace of the Govenors, on the north side of the plaza, is the oldest public building in the United States. It is this building that I work in. I am the Santa Fe City historian.

I told you all of that so I could tell you this. Each Zozobra marionette has a semihard rock-looking, emerald-looking "something" placed in its belly button. It is placed in a cradle holder filled with explosives (an extra amount of fireworks). When the marionette is set to go off, the center really explodes along with the rest of it, and a colorful display is witnessed.

In April two years ago, I was out east of town researching for some historical data on a project the mayor wanted more information on. During that time, on a weekend, Lucinda and I went to visit her sister in El Paso, Texas. We ended up at a flea market where I purchased what appeared to be a Zozobra emerald belly button stone. I brought it back to the office and used it as a paper weight for a while.

Over the next few months, I received numerous comments that it might be a real stone with some value attached to it. Many noticed and commented on how much it looked like the Zozobra belly button. Some passersby even teased that looking at it made them dizzy. Others said it brought them good fortune after they looked at it and got the dizzy spell. Eventually, a reporter from Albuquerque showed up. He asked the locals a few questions, spoke to me, and then had an appointment with the mayor.

The reporter guy was in the mayor's office for some time. I left for home, and they were still behind closed doors. The next morning, I noticed my "stone" was missing. I asked around and eventually retrieved it from the mayor's office. About a month later, the newspapers ran a mysterious article about the strange stone and that this was going to bring "good luck" to this year's Fiestas celebration.

Finally, Mayor Smuther approached me. He and the reporter dude were concocting a plan to help get our city out of the budget crunch. Secretly, the city council approved the deal. The "deal" was to establish a myth around the stone I obtained. To do this, we would create stories about the wonderment of its power and its ability to help people financially. If all went well, the newly created office/committee would endeavor to create rumors and other spins about the powers it gave off (including the ability to heal).

The plan was in full swing. The Santa Fe reporter plastered articles throughout the paper the months before Fiestas time. The television stations even got in on it. They interviewed people who either witnessed or were a product of a financial gain from being in the presence of the "Stone of Zozobra," as it was officially or "unofficially" becoming known.

We could see tourism increasing as we approached the Fiestas time frame. The stone was now on display for all to see and visit. It was drawing a good daily crowd. The local churches even reported members claiming "good fortune stories" as well as increases in church attendance and participation.

The mayor was happy, the city council was happy, and the businesses were happy with the outcome. Record tourism was announced at each business meeting. This meant record profits too! A few televangelists even proclaimed the power of the stone and its healings. The local Catholic churches were more cautious but did declare it *may* have *some* properties relating to healings according to one's *faith*.

But, it seemed, the faithful and the not-so-faithful were prospering. The Fiestas came and went and netted $325,000 more than any previous best year. That was significant! The next year was even better as it topped $500,000 above the baseline from before the Belly Button of Zozobra appeared.

Everyone was in on it. The local Indians would place their blankets on the sidewalks and sell their wonderful handmade goods to the tourists. They were the ones that started making the look-alike Zozobra stones to sell. The stones sold like lemonade on a hot summer day.

The city council approached me and asked if I would loan the stone to the city so it could be permanently enshrined in the community square. I agreed, with the understanding I would get 5 percent of proceeds over the baseline and based on a complicated formula (present and retroactive); the council readily accepted. That meant I would get a check retroactively for the past two years in excess of $41,000. The stone was certainly bringing everyone good fortune, including me. And the checks kept coming every year.

The city council still meets, but no record will be found on the council's official agenda/minutes about the promotion efforts of *the stone*. Not much promotion is really needed now as it self-promotes itself very well. The stories and the miraculous healings continue and are repeated in the media. One can overhear gossip about it at church meetings, coffee shops—almost anywhere one goes. It has become a religious icon as much as a business enterprise.

The doc says I only have a few months left, maybe weeks. And now, for my confession as dictated to Lucinda:

"I really didn't obtain the stone at a flea market in El Paso, Texas. That is the story I told so that the stone would belong to me. The city of Santa Fe was originally occupied by a number of Pueblo Indian villages with founding dates between 1050 and 1150. I found the stone at one of these Pueblo Indian sites during an excavation, and I believe it to be a relic belonging to their ancestors. Further study and inquiry into their history should bear this out. It is my desire that it be returned to them upon my departure."

Oh yeah, about the reporter from Albuquerque ... He was a contact of mine from my college days. Juan Salvadore and I go back a long way. He really has been a good friend to me and my family over the years. Adios!

# Champy

*New Yorkers and Vermonters beware!*
*Champy might be here ... or there!*

We moved from Rochester, New York to Plattsburgh, New York after retiring from our health food business. We wanted to find a smaller place after our four children had left the nest. They were all grown and married, and making their own way now. We found our new life in Plattsburgh refreshing, stimulating, and relaxing.

Plattsburgh had lots to offer us as we enjoyed the aspects of Lake Champlain, which was a border between New York and Vermont. We found the beauty of sunrises stimulating at Point Au Roche, and the prospects of boating excited us too. Plattsburgh even had a nice little Mexican restaurant called The Tijuana Jail, which we began frequenting. For my wife, the life of a day at the mall in Montreal got her thrilled as it was only about a sixty-minute drive away.

Our health food store treated us well while we built it up over the years since the 1970s. Then we sold it! Yes we did, and got a good price for it. But now I found pleasure in fishing and traveling. Yes, I was doing what I wanted to do, when I wanted to do it, and where I wanted to do it—or not doing anything at all! Ahhh, the choices of retirement.

Rona still liked the mall life. So she and her new friend, Crystal, made the trip to Montreal, Canada, about once a month. Crystal's husband, Ben, and I did lots of fishing and boating. We would go with the girls to Montreal occasionally, and then we'd get some fishing in since Montreal has very good trout.

Ben was a gentle sort of man. He and Crystal had a similar career background as Rona and me. They had been in the "healthy eating" restaurant business. And that was the name of their restaurant: The Healthy Eats Dining Place. They left The Big Apple (New York), and they too sold their business and fell upon Plattsburgh, where they obtained property close to Lake Champlain. We lived about two or three miles from them on a wooded lot of about seven acres—log cabin and that sort of thing. It was something Rona had always wanted, and now she had it. She was happy and content.

The four of us did stuff together. As couples, we liked to go to Montreal. The girls would shop, of course. A couple of times, we took a horse-drawn calèche ride through the cobbled streets for a few romantic moments. The scenery was breathtaking as we'd ride along the Saint Lawrence River.

An interesting fact is that Montreal is one of Canada's largest film production centers. Many Hollywood films have been shot there, including *Snake Eyes* (1998), *More Tales of the City* (1998), and *Battlefield Earth* (2000). If you look real close at the beginning of the movie *Battlefield Earth*, and before the story unfolds, you'll see us riding in a calèche along the river. "We're stars!" Crystal and Rona would exclaim to anyone they told the story to. And then they'd add, "Do you want our autograph?"

Maple syrup is in high production there, and the sugar maple is a symbol of the area. Maple syrup goes well with hotcakes or pancakes or "cakes"—whatever you prefer to call them. To me, a rose by any other name is still a rose, or a carrot, turnip, etc. Ben and I entered the annual cake-eating contest once; we didn't win but did have some good "cakes."

It was Ben who told me about Champ or "Champy" as the locals called him (or, *it*). The creature is reported to have been seen hundreds of times in the lake. Many compare the legend of Champy to that of the Loch Ness "Nessie" Monster. Ben went on to explain that Lake Champlain is 129 miles long and is a deep, freshwater lake. Champy could easily hide in the lake, Ben would remind me whenever we were out fishing or just boating. "Thanks a lot, Ben!" I'd say.

Champy is said to look like a prehistoric plesiosaur reptile. But these things were supposed to have become extinct 65 million years ago. I did some research and discovered that the plesiosaur reptiles lived in the sea from the Triassic Period about 213 million years ago, until the Cretaceous Period of about 65 million years ago. This is the time when all dinosaurs became extinct.

Now, to clarify, a plesiosaur is believed to be a prehistoric type of marine reptile and not a dinosaur. It had a long, snakelike head and neck and four large flippers instead of legs. After I did my research, I told Ben he was full of it when he'd bring up anything to do with Champy. We had several discussions on the subject and ended up in friendly arguments on the possibilities of such a thing.

Last summer, I decided to make a replica of Champy, take it out on the lake, take some pictures of it, and play a joke on ole Ben. I did a very impressive job on Champy if I might say so, and without much debate from myself. Well, I put it in the back of my pickup, covered it up, and off I went.

It wasn't all that heavy, so I brought some weights along and used them as needed. I rowed out a ways, set it, weighted it, and then tied it with lightweight twine before paddling back to shore. I used my row boat so as not to make noise which might draw unwanted attention in the early morning hours. Dawn was just coming when I took the pictures; got some good ones too. I would burst out laughing as I rehearsed the story I was going to tell Ben.

To make things authentic, I worked myself up and then headed right over to Ben's house and pounded on the door. He came to the door in his pajamas and I laid it on him—real thick. Crystal heard us talking and came from the bedroom. I retold the story to her; they both didn't know what to believe. I held up my camera and shouted in my best theatrical voice, "I even got it on film!"

I picked up the roll of film with the promise I'd call Ben and Crystal as soon as I got it developed. Got the pictures developed and back at the house, Rona and I looked at the pictures ... very believable. Ben and Crystal came rolling into the driveway and squealed the tires to a stop. In a flash, we were all sitting around our kitchen table, looking at the pictures.

We were all drinking our coffee while Ben mused over the pictures for the nth time. Then he let out a holler that jolted us. "There's two of them!" he shouted. And again he shouted, "There's two of them! Holy smokes, there's two of them!"

"What are you shouting about?" we all asked in unison. Ben pointed at two of the pictures and said, "See, there's two of 'em—two Champys. Here, this picture is better than the other one," Ben said.

Upon closer examination—and we did examine them closely—we could all see *them*. The first Champy, my faked one, was definitely clear. However, further in the distance and behind and slightly to the right in the upper corner, was a second one—smaller and not quite as visible due to its distance out. Of the twenty-four pictures, two showed a second Champy. I was flabbergasted!

I, Andy, became a believer with Ben and many others in the area. We showed that picture to any who would listen to our story at every coffee and donut shop around. Thousands of tourists arrive each year in hopes of photographing, videotaping, or just seeing this elusive creature.

If you ever come and visit Plattsburgh, stop in at The Tijuana Jail for some good Mexican food. If you hit it just right, you might just see two guys there, or maybe at a donut shop, or any other place in deep conversation, gawking over two photographs. Don't interrupt them if you're in a hurry, but if you've got time and an open mind, approach them very carefully and say, "What cha got there?"

# Mamma Mia, Pass the Pasta!

*__Problem:__ What good is a secret if you can't tell someone?*
*__Solution:__ Secrets will eventually to be told.*

My name is Martha, but everyone calls me Marty. I grew up in a small village not far from Naples, Italy. My mother and dad divorced when I was four. When I turned fourteen, my mom married a United States Air Force sergeant, and about two years later, we moved to Austin, Texas.

My new life in the States would take a little getting used to. Fast foods were not too familiar to me, but I learned to like them, especially when I started mingling with my friends. But my mom was a great cook, so I also introduced my friends to my mom's Italian cooking. I'd be out and about with my friends, and then we'd end up at my house eating leftover pasta. My mom loved anyone who ate her food and gave her a compliment on her cooking.

While mom accumulated her compliments, one of my friends said that a new family had moved into the neighborhood, and she thought they were Italian. Mom then chimed in and verified that was correct and that they had three teenage children. She then suggested we should go and introduce ourselves to them. We all decided we would as soon as we ate the last of the pasta. That's when I met Joe.

Joe was Italian all right, right down to his dark hair and brown eyes. I had just turned seventeen, but Joe was only fifteen. That's why we dated in secret. He was a hunk to me and a gentleman, and I fell for him. I was hoping we'd date for a while and after a few years, our age wouldn't make a big difference. But after a year, I became pregnant.

I told the story that I got raped. My parents bought it and yes, I even convinced Joe that the pregnancy was from the rape. Before I had my beautiful girl, we moved to Omaha, Nebraska, where Chelsea was born after only a few months. We decided to tell everyone that Chelsea was my mom's little accident, so she was raised as my little sister.

I entered a business college and after two years got a job with an insurance company. Ray was stationed at the Air Force Base with my stepdad, but they didn't work with or know each other until they were introduced at a mutual friend's retirement ceremony. That's when I met Ray. He came over to our house to visit often, and he and my stepdad readily became best friends. They swapped a lot of military stories— some true and more made up or exaggerated.

Ray was sixteen years older than me, and he was just what I needed. He had financial stability and a good sense of humor. He had been married in his youth (when he was eighteen, I think) but didn't talk much about that. We loved each other very much, so when he proposed marriage, I sat him down and told him about Chelsea—at least that I was raped, and Chelsea was the product of that rape. I added that if he was going to take me, he must also take Chelsea. He agreed without hesitation.

We married and had a great time together. At some point, I planned to tell Ray the whole story about Chelsea, and Joe, and well, the whole story. When someone is in love as I was, one doesn't want to hold anything back from one's partner. I just needed the right moment.

My conscience played on me, and I knew that "right" moment was coming. Ray was in the den, so I opened the door and saw him sitting in his chair with an open photo album lying across his lap. He called me over and said he'd like to tell me about his previous marriage and family.

He showed me pictures of his wife in their early years, the places they visited together, and the home they lived in. He said the marriage was short-lived, and then he turned the page to a baby—a healthy, beautiful baby boy. Ray said that was his son. The boy took after his mother more than after Ray. The next page showed everyone a little older and was very revealing. I began to cry.

Ray held me and said he didn't mean for the pictures to hurt me. He just wanted to share his whole life with me. I accepted that, and I told him I loved him more than ever but kept the real reason for my tears to myself. You see, when he turned the page, the picture was of a young boy. It was Joe when he was a little older and recognizable. Now, I knew I would hold yet another secret in silence for a long time.

# Moving On Up

*We all like success and develop various schemes to achieve it. All good plans have alternate routes.*

Istarted my career as a checker for Wholesome Food Stores in the 1980s and worked my way through assistant manager, manager, and then district manager. I am currently a regional manager. When I first started, there were relatively few women in management positions. I always wanted to be "management material," so I resolved I'd do anything for a promotion to get closer to my goal.

Mr. Ronald Richardson was the first store manager I trained under. He was an unemotional man, and I worked under him for five and a half years with not a hint of a promotion in sight. He left, and Mr. Robert Sims took his position, while I continued night classes and some online computer college classes. Although a college degree was not required to be a store manager, I believed it could help give me an edge. I finally completed my college degree in retail food services management.

After I had three years as a checker, I began applying for assistant store manager. Each time I applied, I was denied. No reason was stated other than "need more experience." Every time, I would quote the requirements and rattle off the job description to show them that I was qualified, but to no avail: no promotion. I was a determined German gal, and *no* was not what I wanted to hear.

My husband was laid off from his job as a sign maker and found employment at a fast food restaurant shortly after I completed my college degree. A store manager position opened up across town, so I applied for it. This would be my fifth time to apply for a management position. Red "Rooster" McKnight was the person I'd need to convince that I was the right person for the job!

I was hungry for the position, and I was determined to find out as much as I could about the "Rooster"; and I did. My research told me he was a bachelor with several children scattered around the city. He also liked to eat at the best steak houses in the area. He lived on Mirror Drive, one of the richest parts of the city in Detroit. Good-to-know info, but how was I to use it? That was the question. I needed to find the answer and the opportunity.

I prepped myself for the interview. I practiced in front of the mirror, and my presentation was constantly on my mind leading up to the moment of the interview. After I got dressed up, I looked like a prom queen—and my green eyes were stunning, I might add. For some reason, I wasn't nervous when I entered the office. It's hard not to be nervous as I didn't expect to get the job, but giving it my all was what I was about—determined and spunky!

The interview went smoothly. I could tell he liked me, and he was actually very handsome for an older man. The questions were easy to answer, and we talked casually for about thirty minutes, maybe an hour. He then asked if I would join him for a drink. I stated, "I'd prefer to have a nice juicy steak." In the back of my mind, I was thinking, *Where did that come from?*

We did have that drink and a steak at the Steak Barn. Wow, what a nice place! Red made me feel comfortable, and I felt important. I felt more important than I'd ever felt in my entire working career. We laughed, talked about our high school days, and some about his business, Wholesome Food Stores. Then we went to his place for a couple of hours.

The next morning, I got a call from personnel stating I was selected for the management position and that Mr. McKnight wanted to see me at eight o'clock on Monday morning. I told my husband about the promotion, but nothing else. That was my professional career, I kept telling myself, and I was going to keep it that way. If this was how to get ahead, I was determined to do whatever it took to get away from living paycheck to paycheck any way I could.

On Monday, I went to his office and was even more relaxed. I took in the wonderful décor of his office this time. The beautiful flower arrangements I barely noticed last visit were inspiring and breathtaking. The gigantic desk was even bigger, and the couches and matching chair were more comfortable. The air even smelled spring fresh. *I was here and have made it,* I kept telling myself.

I was oriented to my duties in a professional environment, given short briefings from Mr. McKnight's executive staff, and treated like royalty by the secretarial workers. I was even addressed as Mrs. Stafford. Wow! This was heaven, and I was an angel with wings. After that, Mr. McKnight took me to his house again.

I began my duties and was amazed that everything went fairly smoothly. My time spent observing other managers had paid off. Inspections went easily and pay increases were plentiful. And yes, every other Monday, I was summoned to Red's office and then made the trip to his home. Where would it end?

I was summoned to Red's on the next two Mondays, but I didn't show up. The next inspection of my store was disastrous; the report was filled with numerous write-ups. This was upper management coming down on my management. I kept thinking this was unfair and wondering how I could fight it. All I could think about was "paycheck-to-paycheck living." After a monster chewing-out by Red's team, I knew exactly what I had to do.

With my desire to excel, I went to Red's and found him waiting for me. I told him I was a fast learner and led him to his bed. Two years later, I was promoted to district manager. As district manager, my duties included meetings every Monday with Red. Last spring came the promotion of regional manager when Red mysteriously died.

I promoted Fred Stinger, my buddy from my old checking days, to be the store manager of my old store. He was grateful for the promotion, and he is a quick learner. He knows that when I summon him to a Monday meeting, he'd better be there! Besides, he's a good-looking younger man.

# The Visitor

*Some say, "fear is a great motivator." Others say,*
*"the more you know, the less you fear." Still others*
*say, "the more you know, the more you fear."*

His name is Brian. He was very important to me—his family and his story. He was standing on the front porch when a young man approached him and said, "Are you ready?" Confused, he asked the gentleman to repeat himself. The man didn't answer but just reached out and took Brian by the hand. He turned and saw his body lying on the porch near the porch swing where he and I had sat and swung on many occasions. What was happening?

Brian had just encountered his final scene on earth. To anyone who may have witnessed this scene, it would appear he had grabbed his chest, stumbled, and fell due to a heart attack. At least that's what I saw. About two years later, he appeared to me while I was working in our poppy flower garden.

Poppies are beautiful flowers. They come in such a variety of colors; the red ones are my favorites. My name is Lisa, and I was fortunate to have been married to Brian for fifty-four years. He told me of some interesting things when we had our last encounter in the garden.

Over the years, Brian and I had many heart-to-heart conversations about life, love, and the afterlife. These discussions reduced concerns over such matters and connected us as well. However, his imparted insights on the enlightened *visit*, are a wonder to me. I can only hope to clearly convey as much of it as possible to those who desire understanding.

The visit began by Brian's gentle voice calling my name and affirming his love for me and his loved ones still here. He stated that he had already encountered friends and, in particular, numerous relatives who were assisting in his assimilation into his new environment. He then related the following:

1.  The spirit body looks similar to the physical, but without the flaws. I think that must be why Brian looked like himself, but not exactly.
2.  They eat food (not exactly like ours), but it is not necessary for sustenance. He stated it was extremely tasty and enjoyable.
3.  The secret of godliness is well guarded from full communication to mortals. Brian expressed that to look in a mirror, one could understand the concept of development to godliness or higher beings and their stations. This was to be understood only by deep contemplation and not by the outward communication of inadequate words.
4.  Clothing is not needed in the higher spheres as the spirit gives off a constant, beautiful glow due to high energy levels. However, a robe-like garment is projected about one's energy. For as one spirit being looks upon another, they can feel, touch, speak, and otherwise converse between one another just as mortals would.

5.  I always wanted to know about the body. Brian stated he has a spirit body, which is what I could see, and that his physical body was in the grave and there to stay. This was perplexing, and he perceived that in my eyes. He continued and stated that the spirit body was just as physical as mine in its environment or "level" in relationship to another spirit being at his same level. The "earth" body is what a space suit is to an astronaut. It is only needed in the terrestrial level and numerous planets like this earth were in that sphere.

6.  He further declared that there were many "levels" and that the spirit was and always has been eternal. He stressed that last point. He must have seen I was having a hard time understanding, so he ended that segment of the conversation.

7.  He said that relationships could be everlasting if those participating desired it. Desire and will are very important concepts, for no one is ever compelled in that world. The stronger the love in the relationship, the more likely the relationship will continue in the higher realms. However, spirits are limited by the level which they temporally attain and live in until they progress into the next level. He emphasized the word *attain* as if we determine our level of existence by choices, desires, and our willingness to comply in all of our phases of existence.

8.  What about animals? Brian smiled and only established he was not at liberty to expound, but they had a purpose beyond earthly needs, and some human writings had fairly accurately speculated their true and full purpose. Seek and you will find the answers to all questions.

This is all I care to relate at this time. I'm getting elderly and require more rest than I used to. I do strongly desire to be with Brian someday soon. We had a great marriage and raised three beautiful children: Landon, Brayla, and Tyler.

What's that you say? Yes, sir, I think I'm ready.

# Where's Jenny?

*We work with all kinds. "We" are all kinds.*

It sure is pleasant walking down this tree-shaded road. It's quiet but not lonely. I enjoy being alone at times. The quietness that comes with it and my thoughts keep me company. I used to stroll here with my wife, Jenny, but she's since departed. I had it planned that I would go first, but it didn't work out that way. Hey, Jace, stick around and I'll tell you more.

See that old farmhouse over yonder? Jenny and I used to own it, and we raised our family on that land. We had chickens, a couple of good milk cows, a horse for plowing, and a fish pond. It was a good life; lots of memories in there. Ya see it don't cha? Hey, feller, slow down just a bit. I got more to tell you.

You can't see it from here, but just on the other side of that small hill, and about a quarter of a mile more, is where Sam and Dovey McRandle used to live. Their property joined our land, and we used to have some fun card-playing times together. They've since passed on, and one of their sons works the place now. I think his name is Logan. Wait, I got a pebble in my shoe. Stay here while I dig it out … thanks for waiting.

Hey! Sam! What the heck? Dovey, you're looking pretty as ever. Okay, be that way and don't say hello. Stuck up! Jace, can you believe Jenny and I were friends for decades with the McRandles, and now they won't speak to me? … I hope they rot in hell!

Sam the butthead! That's what I thought of him all of those years. He had a good-looking wife and didn't even appreciate her. Dovey was the Turkey Trot Queen of the year in 1958, but they're dead now. … How could that be? I just saw them. Wait a minute. … Oh well, I'll just keep on walking. Come on. Keep up with me if you want to hear more. And quit looking at me in that odd way. You look as if I'm crazy!

Just around the bend in the road is Lester and Brayla's place. There's ole Les now. Good to see you, Les. Well, okay—don't shake my hand! No! I'm not a killer! Why would you say a thing like that? I don't care what you say, Jenny died of cancer, you old lame goat. Scat like the rat you are! Get out of here, dirtbag! Come on Jace, I want to get back to paradise.

*Oh look, it's Jenny! Isn't she pretty?* "Jenny, you look lovely today."

"Hello, I'm Nurse Brown. I can be Jenny if you like. Come on and let me help you up the steps to Paradise Mental Health Sanatorium. Your room and a warm bath are waiting for you, Mr. Wood."

"Thank you, Jenny, you look beautiful. … Did I say that already?"

"We'll take good care of you, Mr. Wood."

"Betty, you're the greatest. That young man that went on the walk with me, he's not very friendly and doesn't say much either."

"Oh, Mr. Wood—"

"Please, call me Jim."

"Jim, don't you worry about him. He's just an intern trying to finish his college degree."

"Thank you, Jace. I'll take Mr. Wood ... excuse me, Jim ... from here."

"Hey, Jenny ... remember our old farm? With the chickens, a couple of good milk cows, and one of the strongest plowing horses around these parts, and the fishing pond—"

"That's some story, Jim, but I've heard it before. You told it to me just yesterday. Now, let's get your clothes off and jump in the tub. Where's Jenny now?"

"You're Jenny! But, you're supposed to be dead!"

"Well, I'm not Jenny, and I'm certainly not dead. ... Stop! You're hurting me! Let go! Ugh, you're drowning me! You're ... ugh ...ugh ... ugh ..."

# Wealthy Lady

*Some like it hot, some like it cold, and some like to be told. How do **you** make your choices?*

You may be surprised when I tell you that I used to be one of the wealthiest persons in Harrison County. Now I'm elderly, gray-haired, and tired. I'm just an old lady who likes to rock in my rocking chair on the front porch. I like my house in the country setting in Mississippi, not far from Biloxi.

It gives me pleasure to see the rabbits and deer that dart here and there, and all the other creatures that keep me company. I've got birds that sing to me too. The cardinal, the chickadee, the mockingbird, and the dove all make a great combo. The woodpecker occasionally provides a good drumbeat to complete the band that even the rock group, The Beatles, would envy. The likes of the blue jay and the red-winged blackbird provide an aerial acrobat show that's hard for the US Navy Blue Angels to compete with. Come on over here, and I'll tell you something of a secret that most around here don't know about.

Ahhhh ... this is the land of cotton, where old times are not forgotten. I grew up around and near Shreveport, Louisiana. My father was a monument maker and sculpted grave stones. His works appear in some of the most prestigious graveyards in the state of Louisiana and beyond. He sculpted beautiful angels, headstones with magnificent engravings, and gothic-era creatures. His works were sought out as he developed his business and his name and reputation spread. We became wealthy in time, and this related to my popularity in school. I dated the most popular and well-to-do boys through high school and after.

I was voted "Most Popular," and I was. I won "Miss Black Beauty Queen" the year after I graduated from college. In college, I excelled and graduated with a 3.86 grade point average, majoring in economics. It was in my last year of college that I met and began dating a handsome young man named Josh Miller. We fell in love, but there was just one concern: he was not a man of color.

My brothers and some of my cousins couldn't stand the thought of my dating Josh. He couldn't come to the house because they harassed him and even roughed him up a bit last time he called on me at our "growing up" home. My dad didn't care for their behavior, but my brothers were difficult to control. So Josh and I met at other places and really enjoyed our time together.

I recollect that I was a lot different from my brothers and younger sister. They were so narrow in their worldview and were lacking in a more broad perspective of life. I wanted more than just a steady paycheck to run around with beer-drinking, cigarette-puffin', partying friends. I think they did illegal drugs too. Not my scene, mind you.

Josh and I decided we'd had enough of the hide-and-seek life, so I moved out and got my own place with him. About a month later, we got married. I didn't tell my friends where we moved to but kept in touch by phone. I would stop by and visit Dad at his work. Mom would always show up and be there for my visits. Josh came with me most of the times when his schedule permitted.

About six months later, I was happily surprised to find that I was pregnant. Josh and I were excited about it and went out and celebrated. We relayed our good news to Mom and Dad. They were excited for us. I wanted to share the news with my other family members, so I dropped in one day on them. All I got was a slap on my face, and I was called names too cruel to repeat. I left with a resolve never to return to their presence again.

Josh and I were doing fine after a few years. We had good jobs, and moved into a nice home and neighborhood. Our baby girl, Sonjanique, was starting the first grade. Then we got the news that my parents had been killed in a freak accident. That was heartbreaking.

The estate and money were to be divided up, and we all did well. My siblings and I got over $200,000 each, but my parents left me that plus the business. Five years later, our home got broken into and robbed. The thieves got away with some jewelry, two television sets, and about $350 in cash. Good thing we weren't home when it happened. We had the back door repaired, and Josh installed a video camera. A couple of months went by, and it happened again.

This time, we viewed the camera and found that it was my brothers, all three of them. The problem, according to the police, was that the video tape could not be used as evidence since we hadn't displayed a visible sign stating that the property was under survallience. Naturally, they all declined to talk to the police and denied any involvement—with smirks on their faces and all. But, we knew, and so did the police. We'd all be watching after that episode, and so we invested in a full security system, signs and all.

Sure enough, they came back, but this time we were legit. It's hard to believe they squandered their inheritance away in such a short time. It all came out in court that they were responsible for numerous burglaries over the past ten months totaling over $60,000 worth of stolen goods. What a waste of three lives. They were also charged with the murder of one of the persons they had robbed.

The thing that surprised me the most was that the police connected my brothers with the murder of our parents, and they were convicted of those murders as well! All three of my brothers got a stiff penalty, and they will be serving in prison for a long time to come. And to think, my video brought it all together—their own sister had to assist in putting them away. Not that I'm proud of it, but they hopefully can't harm anyone for a long time—and I do feel good about that!

# Two-for-One Shot

*Intentions, even the best ones, have their unintended results.*

I pen this paper in my prison cell in answer to your solicitation in a magazine I recently obtained. The magazine was over a year old, so I hope you can still accept my story. In 1994, I was convicted of murdering my neighbor and his wife, as well as my wife. I now sit on death row and await my execution, which is expected to be sometime this year. Before my life is ended on this planet, I would like to set the record straight as to how I got here. Please hear me out.

I understand it is not easy being married to a beautiful woman. I know that now, of course, but not when I met and married Ellen. She had the most beautiful soft, long, and curly auburn hair I've ever seen.

Not one flaw could be found on her smooth, creamy skin. Her eyes were emerald green, and her body was strong, semimuscular, and very shapely. She stood five feet nine inches tall and not an ounce of extra fat could be found on her anywhere. There was only one problem: she was slightly slow of the mind.

I was already well off financially and had been working as a pharmacist for over six years when we married. We had a very nice house and lived in a cul de sac, in a fairly private area. All this suited Ellen because she didn't handle stress and would not do well even in a moderate work environment. Just casual conversation with Ellen became challenging over the years as her mental state was slowly deteriorating due to early dementia. She was only thirty-two years old.

She could be as adult as anyone for a long stretch and then be very childlike the next instant. It was wonderful taking her out to dinner and the like as she was a head-turner. Occasionally, however, she would get into a fit—or a tantrum is more like it—if something didn't go her way. Once she got upset at a waitress because the waitress reversed our order when she served it to us. Ellen jumped out of her seat and sat on the floor until the waitress hurriedly corrected the situation. Embarrassing then, a little humorous now, as I think and write about it.

Ellen liked working in the flower beds around the front and sides of the house. Once I drove up into the driveway, and Ellen was on her hands and knees covered with dirt on the east side of the house, planting tulips. As I approached her, I could tell she had on nothing but a thong, a tight-fitting bra, and running shoes. I don't know how long she had been outside, but I rushed her into the house and lectured her on her appearance. She actually thought she had put on a bathing suit to work in.

Well, with all of this, I began to be concerned about what the neighbors might have seen, if anything, and what things may have happened or might happen when I was not around to monitor her condition. So I installed cameras around the house; inside and out. On weekends, I would view the latest week's activities. Some things were very humorous, and I fell in love even deeper with Ellen despite her problems and immaturity. Ellen was very loving and affectionate.

Yes, Ellen was a loving and affectionate woman, but one day, while viewing the cameras' weekly activities, I noticed that I wasn't the only one that liked looking at her. Unknown to Ellen, our neighbors across the street had noticed her habits and unusual outdoor attire. The video camera showed we had some Peeping Toms. Not only did they peep, but they took pictures of Ellen when getting out of the shower and walking around the house. I shared this with Ellen so she could take precautions.

One nice sunny day, I went over to introduce myself to my Peeping Tom neighbors. I didn't let on that I knew of their secret activities. We just talked about nothing. Come to find out that Rudolf (he preferred "Rudy"), had been a druggist. When asked what he did now, he seemed vague. I found out later that his license had been revoked, and he was making pizza at a local pizzeria. His wife, Sance, was a pharmaceutical sales representative.

A month later, I was viewing my camera and was shocked at what I saw. The camera showed Ellen opening the door, and Rudy and Sance entering. Rudy handed Ellen a tall drink in a flowery glass, and they all drank from their glasses while talking, laughing, and sitting on the couch in the living room. Suddenly, Ellen went limp. Sance immediately grabbed the drink while Rudy got hold of Ellen and eased her down on the carpeted floor. While Rudy took Ellen's clothes off, Sance closed and locked the front door and checked all the other doors and windows.

Sance returned and was disrobing while Rudy was having sex with Ellen. Sance then joined in. After it was all over, they cleaned up, dressed Ellen, and sat her back on the couch. When Ellen came around, they pretended that Ellen had fainted and that Rudy had gotten her back by administering her some pills. Ellen was not the wiser and would not have ever found out if I hadn't had my camera on them.

I suppose you can figure out the rest of the story. So ... I bought a gun. Then one day, I told Ellen to call up our neighbors and invite them over with their special drinks. They came all right, and were very surprised to find me entering the room about the time Ellen was out and they were undressing. One bullet to each of their heads! Rudy went down first. You should have seen the look on Sance's face when I pointed the gun at her. It reminded me of something out of a horror picture. She messed her pants; I smelled the odor before I pulled the trigger. I guess it satisfied me and made me feel that I was getting even. I don't really know. It was all blurry after that.

One thing I didn't figure on was the bullet going through Rudy *and* into Ellen. And yes, I deserve my punishment; but I have had my say. You now know what happened. My only regret is to Ellen.

# I've Been Around

*Got something of value? Who'll give me $5, $10, do I hear $15? Sold! There are some things you just can't buy or sell.*

I'm doing well, little lady, and thank you for asking. I hope you're doing fine too. I'll start by stating that I'm 102 years old. So don't get smart with me 'cause I can tell and teach you a thing or two or three, ha, ha, ha. Why, my father met the likes of Marie Curie. You know, the one who discovered radium, which is the luminous secret of matter. My father knew her as Manya as she was known in her youth. Some may know her better as Madame Curie. I also have a few secrets of my own I would like to share with you all as well.

While I was a barber in Missouri, a middle-aged man from off the farm would come in for haircuts for himself and his young son. He had a young'un, about ten or eleven years old, who could draw really well. The little chap was fascinated with farm animals and would sketch various animals and farm life. I would barter for his sketches in exchange for family haircuts; he was that good! He was a delightful young feller. He later became a very famous young man out in California. His name was Walt. Yes, Mr. Disney had a fine son. I owe a lot to that family as years later I sold just one of those sketches for over $80,000.

With money in my pocket, I was able to travel, and travel I did. As circumstances would have it, I ran into a good-natured fellow who was in the Mediterranean; sent there as a recovering French Navy pilot from a near-fatal car crash. When I was on the beach, I found him coming out of the water, and he looked curiously odd. I inquired, and he related that he was exploring the clear warm waters wearing special glasses which he called goggles. This invention, goggles, by this man made a great contribution to the science of hydrospace during World War II.

After talking with him for a while, I became convinced he was going places, so I contributed some money to help him get started on some of his ideas. In 1943, Jacques made his first historic dive with a portable self-contained underwater breathing apparatus, also known as SCUBA. In the 1950s, he designed deep penetrating, one- and two-manned submarines and later pioneered projects in long-term underwater communal living.

Already the winner of several Emmys and Oscars, he founded "The Cousteau Society" in 1973, which is dedicated to educational entertainment and underwater research. Why, he could do almost anything when it came to the water. He was a marvelous person, and I have prospered tremendously since my initial financial investment with him.

While visiting my son and his wife in the mid-1950s in Fairmont, Indiana, they took me to a picture show. The show we watched was called *Rebel without a Cause*, starring James Dean. I was impressed with the message of the picture—troubled youth and that sort of thing.

Excuse me little lady, but could you hand me that box of tissue over to your right? Thank you.

Well, back to my story. As I was saying, I was impressed with the picture and was surprised to find out that James grew up nearby on a farm with his Quaker aunt and uncle. My son attended some social functions with the uncle, so we drove by and even went up to the house. To our surprise, James Dean was there visiting as he was on a short break from filming *Giant*. We were very cordially invited in. He was a nice fellow, but somewhat quiet. After we talked, he became relaxed and much more open. This was a treat, and I'll never forget this young man. He handed me a keepsake—a replica key to his car, a Porsche Spider 550. He gave these keys to fans as a memento. See, this is the key! We thanked his aunt and uncle as we waved good-bye. I was hurt to hear of his being killed in a car accident soon afterward.

Back to traveling again … I like to travel, you know. I was attending a Chicago Bulls basketball game in Los Angeles in 1985. The game was wonderful, and a very talented basketball player by the name of Michael Jordan was superb. Michael could leap higher and sail farther than anyone I had ever seen before. He scored sixty-three points that game. At one point, he jumped so high he landed right in my seat. I spilled my drink and got mustard on my shirt from my half-eaten hot dog. Shortly after the game, Michael took off his shirt and handed it to me and said he was sorry. See, there's his shirt on the wall; I had it encased. Pretty nice, eh?

Well, we better end this interview here for a while, little lady. I'm old and tire easily. Let's get together tomorrow, and I'll tell you many more of my meetings with famous and some not-so-famous people. For now, I need a nap.

Note from the interviewer: Mr. Barthalamue "Bart" Johnson died later that day during his nap, as I learned upon my return the following day. I only regret we were deprived of knowing the rest of his rich life.

# Can You Give Me an "Amen"!

*Followers need a leader. Leaders just want
to lead. Watch out for that ditch!*

I only wish you could have been there! That's right. Nobody ever thought it could happen the way it did. I even had my serious doubts. But it did. A miraculous vision burst on the scene, that is, on the pulpit of our believing congregation. We were blessed to see angels appear right before us. I'm not lying! Some later claimed it was Peter and Jesus. Others cried out that the two were Mary and the other Mary. I really don't know. I got confused when different groups declared different beings. Now, I'm not so sure how many there were—maybe a half dozen. But then I was only eight years old at the time.

The pastor told the congregation to go to the community and tell them what they had seen and declare it to them one and all! We did, and our numbers more than doubled in just three weeks. We were reeling as God's people. From then on, and for some time later, we barely had sermons. We would meet and sing and even dance in the aisles and also up on the pulpit, the pastor's sacred area. It had been off limits to all but him, the choir, and the two senior "elders." But no more; we were all equal for a while, and this vision made us that way.

My father was elevated to a lay minister soon after the vision, only answering to the pastor. We had moved to the community of Beaumont, Texas several months before. Dad had been employed by Disney as an animation technical specialist for several years but lost his job when Disney began catering to gay people. My dad had heated dialogs with management and was eventually told to leave or let it go, I'm not sure which … anyway, he left. That's the kind of guy he was.

We found ourselves living next to his parents who were staunch fundamentalists and proud of it. Since I have matured, I call them Pharisees whom the Scriptures condemn as too strict and narrow-minded. You couldn't convince them of that. I clearly see that shortsighted people don't see their mental-midget stature. I suppose if they did, they'd change, and they wouldn't be that way anymore.

Dad had acquired some animation equipment (I don't know where he got the money for it all) and had set it up in the basement. To make ends meet, he contracted out his skills and did quite well. Soon after, the "visions" began at the church as he and Pastor Williams had long get-togethers after church. Dad would not talk about the meetings and would just say he was discussing the Lord's business when questioned.

We didn't just have one vision; we had a number of them. Within six months, we had the third largest church attendance in the area. We had bigwig church people visit us almost every Sunday. They announced that it was time to expand, and we did. We didn't move into another vacated church building; we built our own from scratch, from the ground up. The new church had much more room in the pastor and choir areas, with nice cabinetry for all they needed, and there was equipment that made us a more "progressive" modern church.

Well, that was my informative growing-up years, and I was very gullible. Since then, I have added some "Sophia," that is to say, understanding. *Sophia,* historically also meant "wisdom" and was called "sayer" or "sayings" and "word." In Greek, it was "Athena" as the goddess of wisdom in the feminine. These "sayings" or "logia" (logo) are the mythoi (myths) of still more ancient Egypt. The mythoi are claimed to have existed before and were forbidden to be written down for a very long time.

These "sayings" were oral teachings in all the "mystery schools" ages before they were written down. Some are so ancient that they are the common property of many nations. The Buddha—actually there have been many Buddhas over the many years—expressed the third commandment as, "Commit no adultery: the law is broken by even looking at a wife of another man with lust in the mind." This was written hundreds of years before Jesus expanded on it. Amazing isn't it?

Also, Krishna said, "I am the Light, I am the Life, ... I am the beginning and the end." This was spoken many, many years before Buddha or Jesus and can be traced through ancient Egypt and beyond. Similarly, the story of the rich man who was commanded to sell all he had and give to the poor, is told by Buddha first and later by Jesus.

I suppose you have figured out my dad's role in "the visions" by now. Hard times came to us after he and the pastor were ousted for their part in the fraud perpetuated on the innocent church victims. The church leaders found out and released those responsible. Of course, no money was returned to the giving congregation as few ever found out the full truth of the matter.

Hard times didn't last too long as we up and moved to Minnesota. Our neighbor of just down the street was Pastor Williams—a gentle old soul he was too. Dad made sure he transported his special animation equipment for immediate use as needed. This Minnesota congregation was easier than the one in Texas. Here goes the wool again!

# Germs! Go Away! Come Again Another Day

*Learning was most fun when I wasn't forced by necessity, or by law, to go to school. My greatest and most satisfying knowledge has come after college, and my preschool years helped condition that more than anything else.*

Ever get tired of the way you live and desire a change? A thief, a fraud perpetrator, a harmful jokester, call me what you will, but I'm through with it all. It gets you nothing … except trouble. Oh, I had my fun with rude and critical comments, but I realize I hurt too many people and some I really cared for.

My first persistent cruel behavior that I recall comes from my youth and involved our neighbor; Old Man Rivers. After dark, I'd go over and turn his water hose on. Sometimes he'd catch it and turn it off before going to bed. But on occasion, it would run all night. It was cool. During the cold winter days, his yard would ice over, and it would kill some of his plants as well. I was bad! It sure was fun sliding on it though.

At school, I was one of several class clowns. Ya see, there was this girl named Marlene in my fifth grade class. Yes, you know the one. She had braces, was a foot taller than anyone else, and overweight. And did I mention how ugly she was. I started counting the pimples on her body one time and lost count at 127. No one wanted to be next to her in line, and I pity the soul who didn't know when getting a drink from the water fountain that Marlene had the last sip from that fountain. That person was ribbed for the remainder of the week.

I never had Marlene's germs very long. As soon as someone came over and passed my desk, I would wipe their hand in passing and say, bending over and in a low voice, "You got Marlene's germs." Or if no one was passing by then, I'd get up and go to the pencil sharpener and I would find someone to pass the germs on to. If anybody tried to pass them to me, I'd wipe them back on 'em … or someone close to me if I wasn't fast enough … or the next poor soul walking by. And if I couldn't get somebody real quick, then I'd make another trip to the pencil sharpener and would wipe down someone across the room. What a game we played at poor Marlene's expense. I now wish I had been more sensitive to Marlene's feelings.

That was elementary school. I didn't hear about or see Marlene until high school years later. And that was only in passing in my senior year. I was walking with Randy and Richard, my two best friends back then, and we passed this nice-looking blonde. I whistled and smiled, and she smiled back. I lost her in the crowd.

Randy got closer to me and said, "Do you know who that was?" I said, "No … but I'd like to know who she is!" Then he began to taunt me and said it was "Marlene … lovely Marlene." I called him a liar, but then Richard added, "Yes it really is Marlene!"

We talked several minutes about how we treated her back when and now how we regretted it. Then Richard reached over and touched Randy playfully and said, "You got Marlene's germs." Then I reached over and touched Randy and said, "No, I've got her germs." This went on for several minutes with laughter and scuffling among three friends just having a good time between high school classes.

Well, time went by, and I graduated from college with a business degree and lost track of Randy and Richard. I got on at a local electric company in the business and accounting department, keeping the books. After working for five years, I transferred to the parent company in Oklahoma City, Oklahoma. Six months into the new job, and I met a gal by the name of Karen. Karen was dark-haired, nice-looking, tall, and had a pleasant personality—just how I like 'em. By our seventh date, we knew we were in love.

We got engaged and she had met my parents; now it was my turn to meet hers. We drove the three hundred miles to her parents' home and were greeted at the door by them. After some conversation, I was introduced to Karen's sister, Marlene. That's right. Marlene is now my sister-in-law since Karen and I got married three months ago.

I've had a few conversations with Marlene, and she claims she barely remembers me from school, but I really don't know how much to believe her. She has grown into a beautiful young woman with a nice family of her own. Surprises on top of surprises—her husband is my old school chum Richard! That was a special treat to renew my friendship with Richard as a brother-in-law. I'm very proud to be married to Karen and to have Marlene and Richard as in-laws.

I no longer play harsh jokes on others at their expense. I've learned my lesson. My jokes and pranks are now toned down to more moderate, acceptable social situations, but I still like a good joke. Do you know any?

# The Domestic Life

*We all struggle to get ahead. Some have more help than others. I want all the help I can get!*

Rossario is my flame. I'd do almost anything for him. He is handsome, about an even six feet tall, dark-haired, and I called him my "Italian Stallion," as his family really did come from Italy. I was very much in love with him. Maybe, in retrospect, I perceive I was a bit too much in love. See, when one is in love, one's thinking may not be exactly correct. I have obtained these great words of wisdom now, but have only recently acquired them.

We knew each other in the lower grades but really started liking each other in our senior year. We dated most of that year and then found ourselves working at a local motel. He worked the desk while I was the assistant manager of the restaurant. I'd sneak food to him when I could, and then he started demanding more and better food too! I didn't see the next step coming, but it came anyway.

We were closing and I was left counting the money, when Ross came over to the double door that separated the restaurant from the desk area. He approached and asked me to give him a couple of twenty-dollar bills. I handed them to him, thinking he'd pay it back at a later time. Before I could say anything, he was walking back to the desk area and out of voice range.

What was I to do? I searched my pockets for some cash but only found a few dollars, so I fudged the books by the amount that I gave to Ross. I didn't want to make a scene there, so I finished my paperwork and went home. The next day I was with Ross and eventually decided not to say anything to him. I just let it pass since I'd fixed the problem.

A few days went by, and I thought I'd treat myself to a twenty, so I did. And then I did again and again and again—and then I went to the fifties. With both of us working and with my added income, we moved in together. A few months later, Ross got fired for the theft of a couple of radios from the motel, so I curtailed my enterprise.

With Ross and his situation, a strain was put on our relationship. Ross began to push me to get money from the restaurant. He didn't know about my previous little "business," and I had recently refrained from that for fear of being spied on. I wanted to reduce the possibility of getting caught. Since I had to watch my steps, I refused his request.

One night I dreamed Ross and I became big-time robbers like Bonnie and Clyde. It was sort of strange because I woke liking the feeling, as if we had accomplished something great—and the popularity and notoriety was a great rush too. When I woke up, it kind of scared me to think that excited me. I dwelled on it, and then I came up with a plan.

I shared the dream with Ross, and he liked it. So every evening we practiced "the plan." I got euphoric each time we successfully practiced and completed the plan. Then the night came for implementation, but we got cold feet and scrubbed the plan for that night. More practicing, plus two weeks later, and we knew it was the right time. D-day was fast approaching, and I was hyped.

I was closing the restaurant as usual; it had been a busy Saturday. As planned, Ross came in and ordered a drink at the bar. He was hardly noticed by anyone, as the barkeep had only been working there a few weeks. Ross slowly finished his drink and headed for the restroom. In the restroom, Ross donned a change of clothes and added a beard as well as a touch of gray color to his hair. The restaurant was closing, and the bar customers had dwindled down to a few.

I put the deposit bag with the money and paperwork on the desk as planned. I was several feet away from the money, talking to the manager, and again all was going according to the plan. From across the room, gunfire was heard—that was unplanned—well sort of. From the opposite side of the room, Ross calmly walked out with the money, practically unseen.

Well, that last part was partly unplanned. Ya see, Ross was to fire a shot, grab the money, and then run out. An added bonus was when a jealous woman came into the lobby and shot her two-timing husband. Ross picked up on the timing and took his cue. It worked out better than planned. The couple got the blame for the robbery as well, and we got away with over $8,000. The authorities never were able to get the couple to divulge the third party—I mean, how could they, ya know?

Well, it's amazing how a little something can help a whole lot. That money helped us get over our rough spot. We reformed, and Ross is now a manager in his seventeenth year of an Albert's food store. We have a nice home, and I'm a stay-at-home mom with two teenage daughters. I very much enjoy decorating our home during the holidays. I'm glad our Bonnie and Clyde days were short-lived, because I love Ross, our two girls, and the domestic life.

# Haunting Experience

*I like new and exciting experiences. I also like some predictability.*

Hi! I'm Belinda Jo, and I had an unusual situation that changed my life in my younger days; ya betcha it did! It was exciting and scary at the same time, don't cha know. Put your ears on, and I'll lay it down for ya the way it happened.

I was born in Bemidji, Minnesota. After I turned two, my family moved and I grew up in Bismarck, North Dakota. I had the usual high school experiences, went for two years to a junior college, and then got married to Frank. Yaw, we did, and a year later we had Charlie. We were tickled pink … well, I guess we were tickled blue, since Charlie was a boy. We were a financially struggling little family, but happy we were.

Three years passed, and we got word that a widowed aunt of Frank's had passed away and left us, of all things, a small but productive farm. The farm was just outside of Minot, North Dakota; don't cha know. So we went and visited the place. The house was built in 1937 and was still sturdy as ever. The inside was well furnished and really was pleasingly decorated, but kinda generally run down on the outside. Frank's aunt, Ethel Gates, just couldn't keep the outside up in the proper maintenance it needed, due to her advanced age, ya know.

Our intention was to go and put the place up for sale. On our arrival, we met Pete and his wife, Christina, but we called her Tina as she insisted. They had the cutest set of twin girls; Cassadi and Cammi. They were a sweet couple, only a few years younger than ourselves. Pete asked us to not sell but let him continue to work the place as he had with Ethel. They lived in the small two-bedroom house on the acreage.

We went back to Bismarck, and after assessing our situation, Frank and I decided we'd move to Minot and allow Pete to continue to work the land and split the money that came in from the small cattle herd and extralarge garden. Ethel had met Pete only seven years before, and she seeded the herd with some money, and Pete worked the herd up to over thirty-seven head at present.

Yaw, Pete had a knack for working cattle; we could tell right off. Ya betcha he did, and it showed as we immediately felt the benefits of a better life financially. The house took some time to get cleaned, but we got'er done. We settled in, and then the strangest thing started to happen. I say "thing" and not "things," as it was the same thing happening over and over again.

The first time it happened was when I got up about two o'clock one morning to pee. The old farm house only had one bathroom, so I had to go downstairs to the main floor. Did my thing, and just as I stepped on the first step of the twelve-step stairs, I saw what appeared to be something misty white disappear midway into the staircase. I walked up the stairs a couple of steps. I counted up the steps to where I saw it vanish, and it was step number seven.

I immediately turned the light on and … nothing. Must have been my nightly imagination, I thought. Three days later, at midday, I saw it again while passing by the bottom of the stairs, coming from the living room and heading to the kitchen to start lunch. Once again, I identified the seventh step as the point of disappearance. This happened several more times, and I shared each episode with Frank. He said he'd check it out.

Frank checked it out while I was out grocery shopping, and then he told me that he thought it just might be some vapor or condensation escaping from the stairs. He said he pulled a board from a step and found nothing. The next day it happened again. This time it was much more misty and had a human-looking form to it—scary!

After another discussion with Frank, I asked him to show me the board from the step he removed. He pointed it out, and I noticed it was the seventh step from the top of the staircase and not the seventh from the bottom. I then insisted Frank remove the seventh step from the bottom. He did and what do you think? We found an old-looking metal box. Yaw, we did!

Frank took it to the shed and used an ax to chop off the lock. We couldn't believe it. We counted over $55,000 dollars, and there were some letters and cards from Jaron, Ethel's husband, addressed to Ethel. The dates on the correspondence were from 1942 to 1945. We later found that was the time Uncle Jaron was in the army during World War II.

We told our story to Pete and Tina. I described the figure to them, and although they wouldn't swear to it, they insisted that my description of the misty figure seemed a lot like Ethel. We shared some of the money with Pete and his family and grew to know and cherish Jaron and Ethel through their letters. The mist or vapor thing has never been seen again.

This money did help our herd grow, and we acquired a few more acres of land from our neighbors as did Pete and his family. We do enjoy the farm life!

# Wheelchair Willy

*Don't confuse me with the facts; my mind is made up!*

**M**y name is Charley Wheeler, and I'm a winner! Well, I wasn't very lucky in 1987 when a big ole semitruck sideswiped my Volkswagen "bug." The good thing for me was that it wasn't a head-on collision. I would have lost that one in a big way, if you know what I mean. Here's how the whole thing went down.

I was passing this big semi on Interstate 10, coming from Las Cruces, New Mexico, into El Paso, Texas. About that time, the 18-wheeler decided to switch lanes, and we scrapped against each other, which sent me and my "bug" in a whirl. I skidded and then flipped off the highway onto a grassy area off the road. Next thing I recall, I was dangling upside down from my seat belt. I unloosened the belt and slide down onto the underside of the top of my car. I managed to crawl out a few feet, and my legs wouldn't go anymore. I looked around when I heard a loud but partially muffled noise, and then saw the back part of my car on fire. Shhhhhew, that was close.

I felt a stinging feeling on the inside part of the back of my right leg. I tried to get up, but my legs wouldn't respond. Let me tell you, that was a weird sensation. I blacked out, and the next thing I recall was coming to in a hospital bed. I had a couple of operations, went through some therapy, and then, of all things, got the news: I was gonna be wheelchair bound. I told the staff and anyone else that was in earshot of my voice that I'd be walking soon, by golly! Well, a couple of months later, I came to a new way of thinking, and it didn't include walking.

I was twenty-seven years old then, and seven years later, I was still strutting around in my wheelchair. While in therapy, I came to accept my wheels and learned to use them as my legs. I'd play chase with the staff members and got to where I could scoot around corners, desks, chairs, and other staff, fairly easily. I eventually would tire, and they'd catch me. Then I would be wheeled back for my bath and then off to my room for some television and the world of slumber. Well, that's what they thought.

I'd pretend to be asleep, and later, Steve and I would sneak into the gym and have wheelchair races. We got pretty good, and a few nights later, we met Bill who got us into wheelchair basketball. Eventually, one by one, we were released from therapy, but we continued to meet up at the gym each Saturday morning.

Word got out and around, and we soon had a basketball team that was not just good, but "double damn good"! We, the "Wee Willy Wheelers" were number one tournament after tournament and year after year. I was "lucky" enough to have the game-winning shot during a game that kept us in the playoffs one year. That's when I got the nickname of Wheelchair Willy.

We now had reached national recognition and got a spot on the *Late Night Show* with David Letterman for our efforts. The next season, our reputation had grown such that we were the target of every serious basketball contender in El Paso and the state of Texas. We won that season and found that we had a challenge waiting for us from a Dallas, Texas promoter. This was big and would get us further national recognition with backing from the American National Handicapped Council. Wow, we were becoming big-time!

We got in our practice mode and geared up for the "big, really big" game. We obtained information on the opponents and their players and favored plays. We were also appointed a coach by the National Council, and she really knew her coaching stuff. Her name was Leah McCoy. Our regular coach was selected as the assistant, and we were glad for that.

The game began quick and fast-paced. We fell behind, got ahead, fell behind again, and we were down by two points with twenty-two seconds to go. It was our ball with a time-out ... and it was all on national television! We gathered around the coaches, got our play, slapped hands, and rolled out onto the floor.

Our "play" was that I was to bring the ball down as if I were going to drive in and shoot for the tie and send it into overtime, but then I would pass back to Jumping Joe where he would shoot a three-pointer for the win. It didn't happen that way.

We brought the ball down all right just as planned. I then turned and caught Joe in my peripheral vision and tossed the ball to him. It was a perfect play—or would have been. We sucked the whole team in, and there Joe was all by himself. The problem was that Joe had slumped over due to exhaustion.

Well, the ball hit Joe smack in the chest but then dribbled out of his lap and onto the floor. I looked at the clock—eleven seconds. I grabbed my wheels and rolled hard. A screech went up, and the smell of rubber was in the air from my chair. Then I realized my opponent had the edge on me—what to do? Before I knew it, I had the ball in my hands, then I turned around and took my shot. *Shwooooosh!* Three points—game winner!

But a more important win for me was that when I got so excited, I was hugging my coach and realized I was of the same height as she was. Yes, I was standing, and I was standing on my own! With a little more therapy, I have not had the need of a wheelchair since. But wow, the controversy that was caused by the scene of me standing—and on national television! We got accused of rigging the game and the like.

Finally, after an extensive investigation, we were cleared and awarded the title. That was the beginning of the Annual National Wheelchair Basketball Tournament. I now am proud to have good-paying employment as the president of this wonderful and worthwhile organization. Shwooooosh and slam dunk!

# The Swirling Fishing Hole

*I've done some pretty dumb things as a kid ...*
*and some dumber things as an adult.*

I have a unique experience to relay to you. When I was a kid, I used to go fishing a lot with my brothers. We seldom took bait along with us because we'd just use the grasshoppers we caught at the fishing hole. Sometimes we would have to bring our own bait during the cooler wintertime after the grasshoppers had died off. On those occasions, we'd dig in the flower and vegetable garden for worms. We were too poor to afford a rod 'n reel for fishing; just a cane or stick pole was all we needed. We did all right and had a fun time too.

Mom and Dad sure liked it when we'd come home with a mess of fish. It eased the financial burden on the grocery bill. After the fish were all cleaned up, Mom would cook 'em evening after evening until they were all eaten.

The best fishing hole was the hardest to get to. To reach the "swirling" fishing hole, we had to cross Interstate 45 just south of Huntsville, Texas. That's where we lived, in a country house with a couple of acres out back. After crossing Interstate 45 (I-45) and going a country mile further off the west side of that road, you would find our hole. I recall one trip to the hole that gave us all a scare.

One summer day, my older brother, Johnny; my younger brother, Jesse; and I (call me Billy Ray), were on our way to the swirling hole to do some fishing. We were in the process of crossing the interstate. Johnny and I crossed just fine, with Jesse behind. Johnny and I got to the other side and turned to find Jesse chasing a jackrabbit down the interstate.

"Does the boy have rocks in his head?" we both said at the same time. We saw the approaching 18-wheeler coming fast, but Jesse didn't until it was upon him. Our shouts to him must have helped, as Jesse found himself laying flat out on the pavement as the truck went by. It all happened so suddenly.

My younger brother ... dead! *What would Mom and Dad say?* was all I could think about. A mere second is all it took to have these thoughts scamper through my mind as I entertained a discourse with them. But another second slowly went by, and the truck faded out of sight. We refocused our eyes on the spot where we last saw Jesse, and lo and behold, to our amazement we saw him jumping up from the highway, grinning and waving to the distant truck down the road. We were relieved but puzzled.

While we walked to the hole and wiped tears from our eyes, we figured it all out. The truck just went right over Jesse and luckily didn't touch a hair on his head or any other bodily part. Of all the luck! Johnny and I sure gave Jesse a piece of our mind and warned that he'd better not ever pull a stunt like that again. He never did!

Well, we caught our mess of fish and had great eating for a good while after. Whatever happened to Jesse, you might ask? For a while he was a super-wrestling star, and later became a magician and even appeared on several television episodes of *Magic Secrets Revealed*. I became a country singer and had a few hits. Come by and here me sing at Gilly's if you're ever down Texas way. Johnny, you ask? Well, he took over the family farm.

Every summer in June, and no matter what we're all doing, we reunite for family reunions and take the young ones fishing for ole times' sake ... ours. Oh yes, we're very cautious when we cross I-45. If you see us just after we've crossed ... give us a honk and a wave. We promise to wave back. Ya'll come back to see us now, ya hear?

# Behold, a New World!

*As a kid, the boogie man could get in my closet or under my bed, but he could never get at me when I was under my sheets ... or when the light was on. Amazing, isn't it, how things work? I learned lots of weird things as I got older.*

While in high school, Mr. Barthrow, my chemistry teacher, got me and a few other students interested in the higher ideas of theoretical chemistry. We only had a few experiments, but they got our attention. This was beyond the "normal" assignments and was purely after school, voluntary, unofficial, not mandated, not school yet school, work. Well,

I think you got the picture, but if you didn't, we fully enjoyed it! That spurred me on to pursue and obtain a degree in chemistry in 1975.

The following year, I was commissioned as an officer in the United States Air Force. After training, I was stationed at Nellis Air Force Base and assigned to a scientific group which was to conduct experiments of various kinds at a secluded site called simply, S-4. These experiments dealt mostly with theoretical energies, and no, I was not one of the five scientists assigned since, to be hired, they had to be certified and have credentials and degrees that would take several lines to list.

No, I was selected because of my educational background to be the team's administrative executive support officer. This suited me just fine, since I'd be able to observe these mind-boggling experiments—and they *were* mind-boggling! I saw experiments that go outside the bounds of rational explanation. For instance, I witnessed a candle burn for 117 days without a trace or a hint that it was "burning down." Not even a centillion of a degree of any kind was detected that showed that it had burned.

I also observed a medical doctor remove, repair, and then replace a heart from a dog without the use of any handheld instruments—except the doctor's hands manipulating some laser and other sophisticated equipment. This was cutting edge and exceptional! Unfortunately, I was not at liberty to discuss the details with even the scientists or other members. I was also bound by oath not to divulge too much information concerning these experiments. That is why I am careful to give only selected information to you.

On another occasion, I was in attendance when a very well-mannered gentleman addressed the group on "universal travel." With charts that hovered from out of I don't know where, they showed the universe mapped out to the outer limits of space in extreme detail. I don't know where he came from, but it was completely understood he was not from this planet.

One thing I distinctly remember in the presentation, was his stating, "The ability to space travel by the bending of space, is the way we get around in the universe over a vast amount of space distance in a short time—relatively speaking." His words tickled my imagination, and I wanted to know more. I was not disappointed as the next two days we enjoyed his continued dissertation on "universal travel." Later, I was involved in a few experiments which backed up the universal travel theories he purported in his presentation. This was wonderful! All of it, for the next two years, was indeed informative and was a wonderful part of my military experience. That's all the time I was allowed to serve at Nellis.

One final story and then I'll stop. The news of the stories you've heard about concerning the major governments of this planet having extraterrestrial vehicles—they're true. We do have scientists and engineers assigned to "back-engineer" these vehicles that were deposited here for us to work on and figure out the technology. Our knowledge is progressing, and it's just a matter of time when space travel for the public will be available. I say no more.

I wanted to tell my neighbors, my friends, and the world … but I couldn't. So I tell you and beg you! Please, keep an open mind to things that might be unusual and never scoff at things that are new or different to your way of thinking. If you can do this, a world you know not of, awaits your understanding. Don't close it off, but always seek after the truth!

# The Real Truth about Spring Break '87

*The more outrageous the story I tell, the more people like and believe it, especially in relation to how much they've had to drink.*

S pring break from school was just two weeks away, and my buddies and I were psyched! We planned to stay the week at my uncle's place in Gulf Port, Mississippi, since my uncle was to be gone that week to a training seminar in Dallas, Texas. We would drive from Norman, Oklahoma, and spend the week at the beach, suck down some suds, and watch the "parade of the ladies." Owen Del, Landon, Logan, and I were only in our junior year in high school, but for that week in Gulf

Port, we were going to be known as sophomores from the University of Oklahoma!

That would work well since we were from Norman and knew all about the university, especially since I had a brother who graduated from U of O just last year. Each night for the last three nights before we were to head out on the trip, we would get together and go over the map and plan our trip. It was going to be fun!

We were to leave early Saturday morning, so on the Friday night before, we went for ice cream to talk over our next morning plans and the drive. I had just taken the third bite out of my Rocky Road Delight cone and was crunching away like a madman when I heard a crunch louder than the nuts in my Rocky Road ice cream. I looked out the large window of the Ice Cream Delights eating place and saw a white car plow into another car that I could only partially see from my view.

Owen Del, Landon, and Logan burst out laughing at the "nut" who couldn't drive. Laughing and pointing, we all ran outside, only to be shocked that the other car was mine—the car to be taken on the trip! We were further devastated to discover that my car was also nondrivable. So off to the body shop it went. What were we going to do now?

I was the only one of us who had my own car, and none of the parents would let us take any of their family vehicles. We got our heads together and decided to purchase bus tickets for Sunday morning, and off we went. It took us just over twenty-four hours to get to Gulf Port, which included a few bus stops and a transfer. When we arrived after this unexpected delay, we hurriedly called my uncle's place, hoping to catch him before he departed for his trip and to get a ride there. We were too late, so we spent money on a cab, which we hadn't planned on since our already-limited budget as high school students didn't cover expensive taxi cabs.

We arrived at my uncle's and found the nearest beds to crash on as we were beat. Next morning, we scrounged around for some food. We gobbled down toast spread with some grape jam and downed the last of the milk, then started to plan our day. We all decided we'd walk or ride the city bus system to get around. During the day, we hung out at the mall since it was close, and during the evening, we went to the beach. We saw more girls at the mall than we did at the beach.

What? More girls at the mall! How could that be? you ask. To our surprise, while at the mall, we saw a sign that read "Welcome Spring Breakers—March 20–28." Well, that sent our spirits to sinking. Today was March 17. To our enlightenment, we were a few days ahead of the torrent of girls who would come next week! What else could go wrong? No, let's not ask!

The next day was highlighted by a movie at the mall theater and then the long walk to the beach. By the time we arrived at the beach, we were hoping *not* to meet *any* girls, as we stank from the sweat that poured off of us caused by the excessive humidity. And we weren't disappointed. Friday came, and we relaxed around the house. We watched television and entertained ourselves with some old movies most of the day. We did this to save our money so we could take the city bus to the beach that evening.

The four of us got to the beach and came across a church youth group of about twenty-five people. They were cooking hotdogs with the trimmings around a makeshift beach campfire. We were extended an invitation, and we didn't hesitate to accept. It was nice to have company, and we got all the hotdogs and drinks we could down—and we definitely downed some "dogs." We even got a ride back to my uncle's place from one of the youth leaders. I'd say that was the highlight of our spring break.

On the bus the next morning, we were back on the road to Norman, Oklahoma. We began singing the song that goes, "On the road again, just can't wait to get back on the road again ..." Just as we got started, a girl came over to me and said I looked like someone she had seen before. We compared our backgrounds and found we lived in the same city and went to the same high school. We all got to talking and discovered we'd seen each other around campus but had never really met.

Lexie was her name, and a very attractive girl she was. She had been visiting her aunt Cadence in Biloxi, Mississippi. The more we talked, the more attractive she became. She asked me what I thought about her name. I just said I liked it. What she was really asking me was if I liked her. That bus ride back to Norman was a lot shorter than coming from Norman.

When we arrived back home, Lexie and I dated some. We went to college together and got married in my "real" junior year of college. Whenever we meet new people and get to know them, we relate to them how we met at the wild, wild, wild "Spring Break of '87"—and then we tell 'em the real story.

# Personal Bio

Delbert Doyce Pape was born to Raymond and Verba (Jones) Pape at Hillsboro, Texas in 1951 (fourth of seven children). In the 3<sup>rd</sup> grade his family moved from Portales, New Mexico to San Angelo, Texas and he graduated from San Angelo Central High School in 1970. Del worked at a local hamburger drive-through restaurant in San Angelo called the "Charcoal House"; this lasted from his freshman year of high school until his first year of college at Angelo State University. While attending ASU he met and married Linda Lee (Ward)Benson (first of seven children) of Barksdale, Texas whose parents are Ira(Step-father) and Ruth Ward.

In 1971, Del joined the United States Air force and trained and worked as a Radar Technician. After 10 months of training in Biloxi, Mississippi, Del and Linda took their family for an assignment to Kalispell (Radar Site), Montana for three years. Next followed a 12 month remote tour to Alaska and then a four year duty to Duluth International Airport, Duluth, Minnesota. At this point, Del completed a degree in Psychology from Chapman University and was accepted into an Officer Training School program which led to his being commissioned a 2rd Lieutenant officer. Afterwards, the family saw an assignment to Beale Air Force Base, California for four years. Del and Linda now had five children: Peter, Lisa, Andy, Jace, and Ben.

From California they were sent to Plattsburgh, New York and stayed for two years. Next was a trip to Offutt Air Force Base, Nebraska for four years. While at Offutt, Del completed a masters degree in Public Administration through the University of Oklahoma's "Classroom Without Walls" program. Next came four years at Dyess Air Force

Base, Abilene, Texas and retirement was obtained in December of 1994. While at Dyess, Del spent four months at Riyahd Air Base, Saudi Arabia in support of "Desert Shield/Storm".

After retirement, Del became a Child Protective Services case manager for the State of Texas and served in Baird, Texas in that capacity for two years. Afterwards, he became a certified Special Education Teacher at Wylie Independent School District, in Abilene, Texas from 1997 until 2009. In 2009, Del taught at Goose Creek Consolidated ISD, Baytown, Texas as a Social Studies teacher from 2009 until his retirement in June of 2012.